In the Grimdark Strands of the Spinneret

A Fairy Tale for Elders

In the Grimdark Strands of the Spinneret

A Fairy Tale for Elders

by
Keith Anthony Baird

In the Grimdark Strands of the Spinneret
Copyright 2022 © Keith Anthony Baird

Edited by MJ Pankey

Formatted by Stephanie Ellis

Cover illustration by Elizabeth Leggett

First Edition: November 2022

ISBN (paperback): 978-1-957537-07-8

ISBN (ebook): 978-1-957537-06-1

Library of Congress Control Number: 2022948151

BRIGIDS GATE PRESS

Bucyrus, Kansas

www.brigidsgatepress.com

Printed in the United States of America

Content warnings are provided at the end of this book.

Foreword

With this title, the aim has been to follow the weaving of a fairy tale in its truest sense. As such, all characters have been assigned titles only, and locales have been kept deliberately vague in the hopes, as with stories of old, it may transcend cultures and borders. Now, all that remains is for you to be tucked up in your bed before the telling of it. Enjoy the nightmare …

Prologue

The first stone broke the bridge of her nose. In a certain sense it was a kindness, for its merciless delivery put her on the ground and dulled the onslaught of over two hundred more. One by one, they brought the death of her, and with each strike, the numbness grew as if a drowning tide. A slow, agonising end which thrilled a baying mob, her last breath was a rattle lost in the clamour for her passing. And the crime to warrant such a sentence? Being with child and believing she was in love with a man nearly twice her age. And yet, in her darkest hour, he was not there. While his wife and children walked the grounds of their palatial home oblivious to his betrayal, he watched the girl perish from afar and felt nothing.

CHAPTER ONE

A mother's grief is a visceral thing. The want for revenge is quite another. Together, they can evoke the rise of a primitive passion. But in dark craft, combined with the guidance of one who walks between worlds, these things can be made manifest and become a vessel of retribution to howl from the beyond.

Carrying her daughter's broken body, she waded across the shallow river and slipped into the dense growth of the ancient forest. The one she sought lived far from the eyes of men. In truth, the crone's existence was hearsay, and she did not know if she would find this conjurer before the onset of night stole any chance of it. A cold, grey day, with a chill no match for that in her heart, would bring its darkness all the quicker.

She was wandering with purpose, though with no clear path to who might bring her closure in this. The ache within was the thing which called to the vale's elusive dweller. For hours, she drifted among the ravines and gullies of the place, and many times she would lay the body on soft, mossy banks and double over in a purging of tears. In this way, her mourning soaked the ground of a preternatural haunt and told its warden of her presence. Fauna, too, told the wind her tragic story, which carried its melancholy to the one who was drawn to the seeker. Where water cascaded into a gloomy hollow, she stood waiting for the bearer of broken flesh. With the day all but spent, the last light saw them look upon one another and speak without speaking of the dread that had come.

She was to follow and bring her cold offspring to the site where no saplings could grow. There was a whispered calm here and a lone, fractured bough of an age-old tree which had been dragged to the spot for some hidden purpose. Draped upon its form, the dead girl and the focal point were now bonded, and what was wished could be asked of the necromancer. Asked it was, and rejected, for the tainting of the body was too great, though one glimmer of solace was given. She was to leave. She was to return to her village, to her now empty life and pass the years waiting for a special child to arrive seeking to board with her. A knock would come in the most empty hour of the night, and this gifted youngling was to be housed in the outbuildings with the cattle.

Cradling her sorrow, she departed that soulless place in the knowledge that the bargain she'd made would one day come at a price. Enchanted moonlight set down a path for her to follow, and a nocturnal birthing began. Cut from the corpse, the lifeless infant was administered surgical demonology. The parts unneeded were removed and fed to wild things which came at the crone's behest. These were the offerings given in exchange for 'other pieces' which were grafted to a reimagined corporal shard. An effigy of root, twine, and dark ochre was fashioned with great care and then set to flame with the smoke blown by mouth over the motionless construct.

As the hexen dolly reduced, the incantation was evoked between creeping fumes which slipped in eldritch ways into the nose and throat. And so it came to pass, in the most empty hour of the night, that new life was born from the entrails of death, and its cries were another weeping of the forest.

THIRTEEN YEARS LATER

After more than a decade, the village had become a town of considerable stature within the kingdom. On this, the night of spirit warding, its citizens busied themselves with small rituals such as speaking words of protection and removing personal effects, and the making of talismans to keep themselves safe from dark forces. Fires were extinguished in every home. The sole flame burning sat in an iron brazier in the square where a huge bonfire of sacred oaks was to be lit. In the wake of the gathering, they would take its tongues of fire on torches to their hearthstones and rekindle the cold heart of their dwellings. In this, they hoped for protection throughout the long, dark nights of winter's spectre. Now greying and beyond her best years, she, who had long ago sought counsel with a conjurer, placed wood on her fire in a bid to keep it fed till daybreak. Satisfied it would endure, she took to her bed before the witching hour and slipped into a fitful slumber.

The wilds bade farewell to a lonesome thing which had kept to the shadow regions of the forest since the time of its creation. No human eye had ever spied its form save that of the one who had given it a way into this world. Enchanted moonlight set down a path for it to follow and, in a guise that would endear it to the one it was to seek, it made its way across the shallow river and into the warrens of men. Only the vermin and night-flyers of the place bore witness to its arrival.

In hooded robe, it traversed narrow lanes and found the door of the ageing lamenter. Its intent was a spill of dread upon that threshold, though not reserved for the one who lived beyond that petty barrier. Hers would be a different fate and no less full of horrors the same. It reached to knock and wait for welcome, as the embers in the heart of the home grew cold and still.

A prophecy, foretold by a dealer in death, was bearing bitter fruit from a broken bough.

In sleep and desolate dream, she heard the triple rap on timber, its sound more a summons than request. Snapped awake, she felt a chill so ominous that it belied the cold state of the ashes in the grate. The crone's promise was no longer memory but manifest, and she should rise and give shelter to whatever had come. In trembling footfall, she took to the frontage, unlatched the door with one hand and raised her lantern in the other. A sweet smile sat inside the shadow of a cowl woven of sackcloth, and intense eyes flashed in the wash of light. The girl looked a vision of the supernatural, with long, flaxen hair, and having orbs with vibrant teal irises ringed by a darker hue. Her skin seemed as hoarfrost, and her features the fine lines of a comely rogue. It was a design to beguile and—though laced with fear—the elder led her charge to where the animals were kept, so that the hayloft should become her new and special nest.

"Thank you … Grandmother, this serves my purpose well," she said with a bow.

Her trickling tone brought a shiver, and the old woman gathered her nightwear close and retreated to her home. In desperation, and without success, she tried to bring warmth to the dwelling by relighting the half-consumed wood on the hearthstone. There was no comfort to be found in such a wasted task, and she spent the awful hours to sunrise wrapped in a numbing, nocturnal cold. A bitter remembrance of that day long ago accompanied each wane of an hour. That thing out there, that child but not child, was the spawn of a lust for righteous vengeance. She'd pondered what fate would be hers for the making of such a hateful darling, and yet somehow knew it would be due on the day it would be exacted. When that would come, she did not know, but all the days spent in the company of the would-be perpetrator would see her reminded of the loss of her one and only child. Time had almost healed that wound, so to have its stitches unpicked would be heartbreaking and unrelenting till the score was paid.

Not knowing what else to do, she brought the child food in the morning and set it down on a barrel in the corner. Daylight granted a better look at the girl, and as she descended the loft ladder, it seemed to the old woman that she moved in a peculiar fashion. She saw too that the youngling wore thigh-high boots and as her robe hung from her frame on the way down, it revealed gloves which covered arms to the elbow. They bore no design for the wrapping of individual fingers and had only a fitting for the thumb on each hand.

Seemingly exquisite velvet, they were at odds with the rough weave of the garment she wore. She appeared grateful for the offering of food but paid it no mind and advanced upon her grandmother in a way which made her back away instinctively. The child's strange gait and otherworldly voice were quite at odds with her obvious charm. As she spoke, there was an enchanting innocence to her manner which began to work its purpose on the elder.

"There are things I must have if I'm to make good on the promise you were given, Grandmother. Heed what I seek, and furnish this loft with that which I ask of you. A spinning wheel is first and foremost, and of equal measure, a loom with bobbins, shuttles, and comb."

She paused to ensure the old woman was following every word.

"Shears, so that I may claim the fleece of your sheep, and all the things with which to sew shall also be needed. The pattern for a delightful dress and dyes for its finish will make this arrangement binding and true."

The elder pondered it all.

"But child, I cannot pay for what you ask. The little I make at market by working the land is barely enough to keep this small holding from the hands of the baron, and I would die before I would let that happen."

She almost spat out the words, and the girl understood the hate in her heart.

"Worry not, Grandmother, for I possess something that will make all of this possible."

With that, she reached inside her clothing and brought forth a trapezoid drop of lapis lazuli. It spun on a thread through its tapered end and winked in the light of the early sun. Rare and precious, it would indeed bring all she desired to her loft. The old woman grinned as it was placed upon her palm, and the eyes of the giver flashed wicked in the deal. Within three moon risings the child had her wares, and the tasks to undertake could begin in earnest. As autumn shed its dead things, she took those elements from nature she needed for her special creation. To begin, two sheep were shorn, and the fleece was spun into workable strands. These she soaked in cold water to prepare them for the application of ground madder root, a crystalline powder, and their infusion thereof in hot water. Materials of special tenderness were sourced locally, and the old woman kept her distance as the girl toiled endlessly for seven days and nights. Food left for her disappeared, but the girl did not appear to sleep.

Between loom, needle, and spinning wheel, she brought into being an exquisite gown, the like of which was unique in design and make-up. Each piece of cured hide, of which there were hundreds, was shaped as a leaf of the forest. Its rear panels were a court train which would swirl with each footfall, and a high, stiff collar would envelope a head adorned with twisted hazel tiara. The embodiment of the ancient woodland realm, it now hung on a purpose-built frame and was made for one older than she who had fashioned it. The loft was strewn with discarded materials, and the reek of mortal ruin lay upon it. Near spent, the girl had one last task to perform before the time to slip into sinister slumber would come. And so, she spun once more, weaving another something for a whole other purpose until the darkness crept in through the shutters and became total in the dying of the candlelight.

Chapter Two

Bringing a breakfast of rye bread, honey, and goat's milk, the old woman disturbed crows which had gathered in the loft before daybreak. Some of them scattered as she entered below; the braver few remained and perched themselves on the spinning wheel to caw in response to her greeting. Their presence was odd, but odder still was the fetor which clung to the place. It was a smell she recognised, having put the cleaver to animals in many a year. The rot of innards had a certain stench, and it spoke like no other to the senses. Setting the food down, she inched her way up the ladder on nervous limbs, which might fail her on this morning's revelation. The smell grew thicker with each pass of a rung, and the vision of the grotesque which awaited her slipped slowly into view. The wasted visage of a small boy was the first thing to greet her as she cleared the opening. She froze as the gravity of it took hold, and yet it was soon upstaged by the wretchedness of a macabre scene.

He'd been skinned all over, with only remnants of membrane still attached to hands, feet, and head, as they'd served no purpose. His flesh was drained of fluids, and the birds had ruptured the tissues in search of more moist internal fare. Soft eyes were pecked out, and two small puncture wounds adorned a crooked neck. It would be horror enough on its own, but as just one example among many, it was terrifying. She gazed from each to the next in a loft littered with over a score of youthful corpses. All fates the same, they lay at odd angles and bore the hallmarks of avian attention. And yet, all this was not the worst of it. At the heart of death's destruction, a fat, writhing cocoon hung suspended from the rafters by morbid threads, which vibrated on the pulse of the thing inside. A translucent wall revealed a thrash of limbs within which moved through an egg-white liquid and brought the face, on occasion, to the surface. It was the girl herself in the grip of a nightmarish transfor- mation, one of growth and strange acceleration.

The elder almost tumbled into the space below. She fell against the ladder and slid its length to lie sprawled upon the scattered hay beneath the terrors above. Laying close to an hour, she was oblivious to animals roaming free and the returning crows drawn back to the feast. Her head was a swirl of disaster and woe, of deeds long gone, and of bitter regret. A bargain made was a forfeit due, and this ride to revenge was now unstoppable. *Unless …* She thought of torching the loft. Thought of ridding the farm of the foul resident in the rafters. Remnants of the food she'd brought daily could be seen where the hogs were penned; evidence the girl had eaten none of it, and dined instead on those she'd lured from the township. And lured she had. From field and empty track, they'd followed the 'arcane sprite' on her promise of trinkets and treats. Many would be looking for their sons and daughters … and all would be bent on damnation for the guilty.

Unable to rid herself of so much evidence, she realised the price to pay for her deal with the crone would be the bonfire or the gallows for the lives of the children. It was a doom so large that hers would be infamy. A grim acceptance fell upon her, and she drifted slowly back to the house to prepare herself for what was to come. It had been noted by some that light and strange shadows had emanated from the holding in the most empty hour of the night.

Whispers had become wildfire, and they, along with the notion that the witch of the woods could have taken the children, swirled among the townsfolk. Frantic mothers fanned the flames of suspicion, and soon there were gatherings in the square of those who would seek out the lost. Their mood grew ever sombre, and the promise of vengeance crept into every act and deed. Up in the loft, a whole other thing was growing too, and its want for a payment in 'meat' and screams was years in the making.

As day began a fall away to dusk, activity in the cocoon grew still. It no longer throbbed with hidden purpose, but merely vibrated every now and then in eerie ways. Threads as thick as stout cord kept the sack a good measure from the floor. Beneath, the dress of cured, dyed, and intricately worked skin of youths awaited the rebirth of its creator. Made for a body grown older, whose lines and curves were set for a taller, fuller, womanly form, though still a one of dual assembly. As the last ray of light dipped below the horizon, and when darkness stole in to claim all as its own, a singular black talon pierced the cocoon wall from within, and the pus of suspension began a slow spill. The first of it was foul spatters, followed by a steady pour which dripped through the gaps in the floorboards to form rancid pools on both floors.The prelude to an unspeakable emergence, it was slight in comparison to that which followed.

Morning brought an abandoned loft. Gone too, the wondrous dress she'd fashioned from the leather of babes, with only the ever-growing stench of decay remaining. On inspection, it seemed the hogs had 'cleaned up' something which had dripped from above. The old woman simply shut the shelter and let the animals roam for the day. It was close to evening when the first of the torches, carried by those seeking a retribution, could be seen on the lane to the farmstead. Other things they carried too, such as scythes, forks, and crude blades made swiftly for this purpose in the town forge.

When the horrors of the barn were discovered, she who'd made a pact with damnation long ago was dragged naked to it and bound in screaming protest to a timber upright. Gathered at the open double door, they threw their torches inside and put her flesh to flame for witchery. When wails were consumed by a raging fire, a lone figure watching from afar slipped back into the cover of the bordering trees and seemed as one with the foliage.

A Solstice Feast

A town in mourning for the loss of so many struggled with preparations for the castle's yearly Yuletide ball. To feast and make merry seemed unforgivable in the wake of such crushing sorrow. The shortest day held its promise of a prolonged visitation of the dark, and the celebration's normally uplifting atmosphere was tempered by the grim exhibits from the barn. Though many weeks had passed, the nature of the atrocity would leave scars on a community that would never truly heal. As in years gone by, the festivities involved a vast array of things to prepare. Food and beverage had arrived from every corner of the kingdom and entertainers the same. It was a time of lavish spending by the noble lord and would at least provide a temporary distraction for his maudlin subjects. The sprawling grounds sat under a blanket of snow, and all were made welcome to the stronghold's warmth and splendour.

On the stroke of midday, a lone figure appeared at the outer gate and demanded an audience with the baron. With weak minds overcome by enchantment, the guards granted access, and the visitor took the hidden path to the keep; one known only to family and their elite guard.

As such, peasants and performers alike were bypassed, giving the cloaked soul an invisible arrival. Using the crooked crown of a knotted elder stave, she rapped on the main door of the private chambers and waited. It was a knock on wood which stilled all activity behind it. All felt a dread they did not voice, but a lone servant summoned enough courage to answer.

An ill wind blew in through the open door, and it seemed the same breath carried the visitor over the threshold. She was old and a little bent of shape, yet frailty wasn't a facet of her nature. Smelling of root and earth, she was the very essence of the forest.

The crone, the one they had all heard of yet never believed real, looked from one to another and had them cross themselves in fear. A slight cackle was given to their feeble wards, and she savoured her secret knowledge of them all. Her demand was the company of the master, and she was ushered by one through a grand hall towards the liege lord's tower retreat.

Up a stone spiral, withershins and fleet, they came to a heavy door and rapped thrice to gain entry, and the servant took his leave thereafter. And now, one power stood across from another, for a meeting of gravity to unfold. He eyed her warily, but arrogance would have him see nothing but an old woman with the audacity for an audience. Her exploits were known to him, though he believed the ignorance of peasants had fuelled those tales and lent them great exaggeration. Nonetheless, he kept to caution, and with sword to hand bid her be seated before his questions came.

"What ill wind carries this pedlar of cheap tricks into my chamber?"

His mockery held weight in delusion only. She paid it no mind, for her prophecy was all, and she ignored the offer of his cheap hospitality.

"I bring thee of high-blood born a warning."

At this, he rubbed the jaw which housed a wry smile.

"A warning, you say? And what measures would you have me take when all the realm sits in idle celebration?"

Knowing full well his arrogance and that her proclamation would be met with scorn, she had made the journey regardless, for his rejection of her guidance was all part of the pacts in play.

"Your trysts outside of wedlock are the chink in your armour. Repent and see out many a winter more, or this one shall be your last."

That she should have opinion on his noble entitlements was insult enough, but to stand in his sovereign space and utter it was beyond offence. He'd killed many for far less and that thought steered his answer.

"I could have you hanged, old hag."

"I live not by the petty ways of men. You hold no sway over me, errant lord. Your harms are meagre, unlike those I can bestow."

He weighed his course of action. True enough, he could summon guards and have her executed. But there was something about her manner which stayed his hand. A certain steel in her words spoke of caution and that perhaps not all of the myth about her was imagined.

"Remember well I let you live this day. Be gone woodland walker, and never darken my door again, lest I put my wrath upon you." Simply cackling at his empty show of might, she flew apart in an upward swirl of cawing ravens, which found exit at the tower's embrasures and left a stunned witness to her arcane departure.

A gypsy cart bearing a large, ornamental urn was the last transport to arrive at the castle walls that day. Its team informed gatekeepers they carried the centrepiece of the evening's entertainment. Once inside the grounds, it was taken to a side entrance of the great hall and placed where all eyes would see it amid the onset of a growing blizzard enveloping its venue. The hall was decked with garlands and wreathes, and a multitude of candles brought a dazzling brilliance. A smell of ale and cooked meats gave an essence to the air, and a great, roaring fire projected the sense of welcome. It bustled with activity, for the finishing touches were about to usher in the first of the many. Soon, the grand chamber was awash with the ranks of the commoners and interspersed with a lesser number of special guests. All waited patiently for the lord and lady to appear so that the festivities could begin a-proper.

To fanfare, they were brought before their people when the hour was upon them to make merry. Flanked by their now grown-up children, they took their places at the head table, and the baron's speech got the celebration under way. To great applause, musicians charged the atmosphere with convivial tones, and the masses laughed long and carefree. As the night ran on, all agreed that this year's feast was the best ever, and much needed after the unspeakable doom which had befallen the town.

With drink flowing and seemingly endless food to enjoy, the good people of the vale were putting the dread of a dark year behind them. Far from the castle, on a rocky outcrop at the upper reaches of the forest, the crone pulled her shawl closer and gazed on the bright lights in the distance. A fell wind whipped beautiful flakes of freezing death about her; each a promise of the bane to come. She haunted the moment and savoured it, until, as one with the woods, she made scarce.

In the great hall, the highlight of the evening's events was due to unfold. Dancers took up their positions. The gypsies fine-tuned their instruments, and the nod was given. All eyes were quickly turned towards the wild folk, who jigged in spinning circle around the painted urn. Round and round, their pace ever growing, they played a frenetic tune to wake the sleeping dryad they'd cunningly captured in the earthenware vessel. Bound by their wayfarer magic, the spirit of the forest would perform at their behest on this night of the people, and they'd take a good measure of coin from the baron's purse. It was a doleful melody, peppered with highs of frantic scales which brought an anxious crowd to the very edge of baited curiosity.

On and on the gypsies played, and on and on they whirled. For what seemed an age, they conjured with note and chord and sang in olden tongue. Their dance troupe weaved among the throng and spun on tables of high and low caste alike. In this way, all were drawn into the thrall of it, and when at last the spirit was freed, a collective gasp was unleashed. Rent from inside, a cracked and sundered urn fell away, and the wicked thing within came forth to show itself. As exotic as it was beautiful, it burst clear in a breathtaking flourish and grasped the attention of every onlooker. Dressed in autumn leaves and shamanic root, she spun to entrance her audience and hold their minds ever in the performance. The woman looked a vision of the supernatural, with long, flaxen hair, and having orbs with vibrant teal irises ringed by a darker hue. Her skin seemed as hoarfrost, and her features the fine lines of a comely rogue. She brought a mask of fiery red leaves to her face hypnotically, and used that strange pulse in time with the music.

The baron, previously tired of the proceedings, came upright in his seat and stared transfixed at the performer. He was enchanted. Such a woman he'd never seen, and he decided then and there he must have her. It was a slight not unseen by the baroness, who, shamed, sought pardon, and withdrew from the gathering.

It was well known among high and low alike that the baron pursued whatever he believed to be part of his noble birthright. And so, even amongst those now drenched in the effects of ale, his interest in the enchanting dancer was swift to pass around the hall. Out within the masses, she thrilled all with her wild use of tables and other stout platforms on which she cavorted. Each was a stage on which to steal intimate moments with whomever she saw fit to put under her smouldering gaze. A number of elites were lavished special attention, as were a handful of the peasantry. Even a lone sentry, standing in the wings, blushed to rapturous applause as she made her way ever closer to the one she was intent on. With each encounter, she placed another sliver of envy in his veins and in the many small trysts, flashed her eyes his way to ensure he was ever under her spell.

When finally she reached the head table, she kept her mask in place and met his gaze from behind it; her teal eyes ensnaring their target. Now, seeing her in close range, he saw the full detail of her elaborate costume. Such a strange creation made for a more tempting lure, married as it was with thigh-high boots and gloves which covered arms to the elbow. They bore no design for the wrapping of individual fingers, and only a fitting for the thumb on each hand. Seemingly exquisite velvet, they were adorned with vines and gnarled root, which held fast a simple cluster of toothwort and mistletoe on the backhands of each. The plants' vampiric nature was a symbolism lost on all in attendance, but was the final adornment to a gown which was the epitome of the forest, and crowned with a twisted hazel tiara. In this wondrous design, she was a thing of mystic grace and allure, and the baron was owned by the mesmer of it all.

From one end atop the table, she slinked cat-like along its length, toppling goblets and plates to raucous applause before sliding to a halt before him. The music ceased suddenly, replaced by silence as she produced a flower of sculptured ice from inside her dress and presented it to the overlord. That it had neither fractured nor melted during the prolonged staging of her routine was lost on every onlooker, and more so on the one it was gifted to. A moment passed between them, with his eyes flashing in want for her. Slowly, he raised a hand and took the token, and from the stillness, the gypsies built a frenetic cadence with their instruments, at the end of which, she backflipped from the table and danced away into the once more exploding merriment. The baron's lust went with her, and a last look over her shoulder sealed the seduction. All too much for his daughter, she, like her mother, took the shame of it off to her private quarters.

In a deliberate move, the dancer used the cover of the crowd to disappear from sight and exited the great hall with stealth. Her musicians played on, adding only further mystery to her existence. Left clutching the frozen memento, the baron stood and frantically surveyed the throng in search of her, and then summoned attendants to go find his prize. At the height of the celebrations, he took his leave, eager to hear word of her apprehension. When searches revealed nothing, he flew into a rage at his servants and took to the grounds himself in pursuit of her. The snowstorm howled through the garden tracts and obliterated any prints that would have shown the way she'd departed. He cursed under his breath and, still holding the strangely intact ice shard, turned to retreat from the bitterness of a winter's rake. And there she was … emerging with a brazen swagger from the ornamental shrubs of the landscaped expanse. Against such a backdrop, she was the embodiment of a year's most ruthless season and utterly wild in her portrayal of its destructive beauty.

Wasting no time, he advanced and took her in his arms. That she was willing was obvious by the manner of her lustful response to touch and kiss. Insanely aroused, he would have her right there were it not for her insistence they find a proper place to pleasure one another. Nearby, the stables offered a perfect blend of shelter and seclusion and would be unattended on a night such as this. Once there, not even undressed, they began a coupling, and he slipped between her legs under the cover of her exotic apparel. She moaned in the penetration, but for reasons far more sinister than mere earthly delights. Against a tall, timber upright they put fire into flesh, and she, with her legs about him, began to shed her restrictive clothing. Bare chest now ensnared his tongue and mouth, and gave close-quarter cover to a wicked de-robing. The dress, the thing she'd made from the skin of babes, began to fall apart leaf by leaf and drop to the cobbles beneath in the throes of thrust and grind. Glove and boot, seemingly possessed of their own intentions, slipped off in silent spirals from the limbs they'd covered.

At first, he laughed at the disintegration of the dress, as mares in the stalls began to thrash and whinny in alarm. Theirs was a distant noise on the outer reaches of perception, engrossed as he was in the planting of his seed. He felt her wetness spread across his groin and thighs as they kept a sublime rhythm, but a dawning realisation began to creep in. Through ever-expanding holes in the dress, he caught glimpses of their bodies writhing as one.

It seemed, in these brief observations, her midriff was awash with the oddest of markings. Pleasure distracted him, but, more and more, the thought that something was awry kept threatening their embrace. As if sensing this, she pulled him closer and moaned in his ear to keep his focus on their coupling. By now, the horses were kicking at their enclosures, of which some were breaking at the clasps.

Suddenly, for the first time in all of their embrace, she began to move in a different way. He felt held by arms and legs which seemed in excess of the norm. He tried to come face to face, but she quickly cupped the back of his head and pressed him closer to her breasts. The wetness he'd felt earlier seemed to travel in ways uncanny, and a strange sensation rose to make the hairs upon his body rise in response to instinctive terror. With her head above his, he could not see teal eyes turn luminous green, and canine teeth extend from roof of mouth to hang lower in grisly salivation. Spindly, inhuman appendages gripped him. Each narrow enough to be concealed by velvet and leather two at a time, they now wrapped the originator of a thing half woman and half otherworldly horror. On the cusp of a now enforced orgasm, he screamed in the knowledge that this conquest belonged not to him, but to a hellish creation borne of the crone's portend at their castle meeting.

The horses breached their confines and crashed headlong into a partially open stable door before their combined weight and want for escape from an unnatural abomination swung it fully open. As they fled, she withdrew from his manhood and hauled him off his feet. With two legs wrapped about the timber upright, the rest held him fast with supernatural strength. Suspended this way, he saw the full majesty of her hideous form. Before he could scream again, the thing— half human and arachnid—plunged its fangs into his neck and pumped a paralysing broth into his body. With him limp in mere seconds, she continued the production of the same lubrication which had slicked their coitus in the opening of her abdominal spinneret. It grew thicker in substance to come now in strands which she used to bind him, turning him over and over. And so covered and secure, he was lowered to the ground as she descended to stand on all eight limbs. Retrieving the ice flower from a layer of hay, she cast it out through the open door as a sign and took flight from the scene with her captive in tow.

The loosed horses had alerted guards to a castle conundrum, and in number they made haste to the stables to investigate. To a man they would say what they saw was a nightmare made real. A spider-woman had disappeared through the spindrift, dragging a body behind her on a thread of silken sorcery. By the time they'd rallied and thought to pursue, the storm had erased her passing, and the search for the horror and her victim had been abandoned. Reporting to the baroness, they brought forth the floral sculpture which duly melted when presented, revealing the small object within. Understanding its meaning, she dismissed all but one guard, whom she instructed to make ready her horse. Now alone once more, she examined the old ring she'd taken from the baron's jewellery set years ago. As revellers enjoyed the last hours of noble hospitality on the longest night of the year, the lady of the vale took her horse along a crooked lane to the backwoods for a midnight rendezvous with a seller of souls.

A woman's hurt is a visceral thing. The want for revenge is quite another. Together, they can evoke the rise of a primitive passion. But in dark craft combined, with the guidance of one who walks between worlds, these things can be made manifest and become a vessel of retribution to howl from the beyond.

Carrying her many years of shame, the baroness guided her horse across the shallow river and slipped into the dense growth of the ancient forest. The one she sought lived far from the eyes of men. As winter's wrath began to calm, enchanted moonlight set down a path for her to follow. It was long and winding, and more than an hour passed before she came to the place where bargains were made. Where water cascaded into a gloomy hollow, the crone stood waiting for the ringbearer.

"You shall follow," said the crone.

The baroness was led to the site where no saplings could grow. There was a whispered calm here, and a lone, fractured bough of an age-old tree which had been dragged to the spot for some hidden purpose. Draped upon its form, the wrapped and limp body of her husband awaited and what was wished could be asked of the necromancer. "I ask that you honour our pact of long ago and make him pay for the many betrayals I have endured," said the baroness.

The crone nodded her acceptance and turned her intent to the man. First raised from sleep-death, the baron stirred within the silken wrap and emptied his stomach upon his fine garb. His ordeal was beyond all reason, and the slow realisation of who its perpetrators were began to take hold. In waning delirium, he saw the forms of two women; one old, one less so.

Under enforced resignation, he understood the pact which had been made. His years of infidelity had brought about this demonic agenda. And still, in this moment, he cared not for the slights to his wife.

Producing the ring, the one she'd removed from his personal collection years ago, she would have him look at it. That it was the symbol of their matrimony, and that he'd not even cared it was missing, was the thing which cut the deepest. Of use to neither, she handed it once again to the crone, and the bargain they'd made in a moment long gone had now reached its sombre conclusion. Mounting her horse once more, she left this place in the knowledge her eldest son would inherit the seat of power, and that the crone would send a protector of the land and title to fend for her.

There was history between the blood of crone and baron. He knew not of it, for the deeds which had left her forsaken were those perpetrated by his father. A circle of fortune was close to its rightful ending, and in it, his passing would play its part. Same fiend which had infiltrated his castle, rode his flesh, and brought him to ruin, stepped out from its concealment in the undergrowth. In the light of a single torch staked in the ground, it looked all the more eldritch as it crept in dire intent toward him. In fitful waves he tried to break free of his bindings, but slow and steady, the thing part-netherworld-part-femme took up its final position over his inferior form. It dripped drool over this hateful morsel from canines which began their measured and deliberate extension. Strands of the wrap which held him covered his mouth, and so the creature severed them with a casual rake of a single talon on a foot. To hear his screams in the wasting of him would be rare nectar indeed.

In stealthy acts, other talons razored off the tailored garments which those of low caste had toiled over to afford him his noble entitlements. Chill night was naught compared to the fear icing through his veins. Those screams came fast at first rupture, with the tissues most guilty in the violation of his marriage rent free and flicked to the feet of the crone. Stripped of his manhood and in apt judgement of his treachery, shock and trauma pulled those same screams into silence, as all talons pinned the rest of him down and jaw work began the full disassembly. A focused frenzy centred on the stomach, avoiding vital matter so as to make his end one of lingering torment. Scarlet spray tainted the white canvas of a bitter, frozen ground alongside gorged flesh which fell from a ravenous maw. It was a slow and excruciating death, which culminated in head and spine being torn from a hitherto conscious and breathing victim.

As the crone picked up the offending genitalia and planned its further use by torchlight, she mused that this solstice feast wasn't quite what the baron had had in mind. All manner of preparations she had made to harness the potency of the year's longest spell of darkness. With its final task executed, the crone corralled the creature into the trees at the edge of the clearing and commanded a cocooning once more to bring about a new, and equally horrific, transformation.

As the abomination went to work, a flaming arrow brought temporary illumination to the forest skyline. A gypsy signal, it was an acknowledgement of gratitude to the necromancer for the opportunity to furnish their trove with noble coin. It received a perfunctory nod before she placed the sex organs and the shard of a doomed matrimony into the swiftly forming chrysalis. The ring winked in the amber torchlight before the strands of the spinneret concealed it in their cloaking embrace. It was a sparkle which spoke of an impenetrable sheath that would shield the construct to come.

Neath the watch of the long night moon, she whispered the last threads of an occult binding and took to waiting for a new horror to emerge.

Chapter Three

ord of the baron's demise travelled quick and far, and not all ears were neutral in the knowledge of it. In the north, one who had long sought expansion of his kingdom had always harboured a desire to make those southerly lands his own. Outriders were dispatched, and a testing of neighbouring outposts and patrols would begin. Those of the frozen realm were fierce in their territorial acquisitions, and the baron had fought long to stave off encroachment. His eldest son and heir was an untested adversary, and whether or not he possessed his father's mettle was to be established. War was coming, no matter what the answer to that probing was. The crone, of course, had known this, and had foreseen the dicing up of borders in the dicing up of the nobleman. All was by design and born of an age-old injustice close to her heart. An army would come, many would fall, and in the aftermath, she would stand 'bloodied' and avenged.

Vale subjects now pondered the threat from the north. Some, not trusting that the baron's son could defend these lands, packed up their belongings and took the road through the mountain pass to the east. For those who stayed on, it was a time of deep uncertainty made all the more fraught without word from the ruling household. At the castle, the baroness waited nervously for a promised protector to arrive, whilst her son considered each fresh incursion by the enemy. In the heart of the ancient forest, a fat, writhing cocoon hung suspended from branches by morbid threads, which vibrated on the pulse of the thing inside. A translucent wall revealed a thrash of limbs within which moved through an egg-white liquid and brought the face, on occasion, to the surface. Dark arcana had cooked this new destroyer well, and the crone, pleased with its evolution, took to assuming her role of diabolical midwife.

As day began a fall away to dusk, activity in the cocoon grew still. It no longer throbbed with hidden purpose, but merely vibrated every now and then in eerie ways. Threads as thick as stout cord kept the sack a good measure from the ground.

As the last ray of light dipped below the horizon, and when darkness stole in to claim all as its own, a single black talon pierced the cocoon wall from within, and the pus of suspension began a slow spill. The first of it was foul spatters, followed by a steady pour which dripped to form a rancid pool beneath.

The prelude to an unspeakable emergence, it was slight in comparison to that which followed. Punching through, the form inside tore its cradle apart and emerged with a venomous howl which put birds to flight and fear into all roving wolf packs. It was a sound heard in the distant township, prompting those it reached to cross themselves and take shelter from the coming night.

He was a thing of majestic revulsion. A hybridisation of man, spider, and armour plating, he stood tall in stature, wide in brute strength, and bore a face of handsome death. A vision of the supernatural, he had long, flaxen hair, and orbs with vibrant teal irises ringed by a darker hue. His skin seemed as hoarfrost, and the facial features were the chiselled lines of a comely warrior.

It was a design to evoke fear, and, though outlandish when in open form, looked no different from a fully armoured soldier when all legs were tucked and sited for human guise. The ring's metallic element had provided the ingredient for the all-over tensile sheath, and as the conjurer surveyed her handiwork, she used water from the nearby fall to wash him clean. All that remained was to furnish him with weapon and horse, and so she led the fiend out of the hollow and journeyed to the place where wild predators had brought down a stray gelding.

In the tract of woodland dubbed "The Watcher's Graveyard" by townsfolk, she wandered among the litter of bones with her new beast in tow. After a brief search, she found what was left of the fallen steed and laid a flaming torch on a mossy rock. Dead would become undead, and the forest would replace what had been stripped for sustenance.

In dark art's trance she slipped to be the focus of a space for fell forces to dwell. And she, the conduit, gave rise to a creeping replenishment which gave up sap in place of blood and vines as substitute sinews. Binding to a skeleton half sunken in marsh, these bodily alternatives began to lift the fetid remnants from their dampened deathbed.

Crone and forest were one, and so reanimation was a process which came together at pace. Creepers raced over the frame and hoisted the shell to a standing position. Tall grasses weaved throughout to bring mane and tail, and the density of timber lent its element for hoof.

With bark-like skin, it was a dappled nightmare which reeked of decay and earthy spore. Its skull remained uncovered, and it saw without a refashioning of orbs from the eyeless sockets. Points of unearthly green light haunted both dark cavities and pulsed a slow rhythm within. It reared up on deathless energy to emit a sinister bray which swept through and beyond the eerie hollow. Now, given means of transport, the spider-warrior mounted and was thrice instructed by the crone.

Journey first, she told him, to a clandestine meet with the gypsies for the furnishing of weapons, and then on to the town to put the baron's now rotting heart into a sump of special purpose. Lastly, he was to take his place at the right hand of the lady of the vale as her protector, and await further guidance on matters most dark.

There Came A Pale Rider

Fully armed with bastard sword, battle-axe, and morning star, the rider guided his horse across the shallow river and away from the dense growth of the ancient forest. The gypsies had provided potent steel for the tasks at hand, and the few visible lights of the township were now the lure in the distance. In its need for constant renewal to fuel its necromantic propulsion, the horse drew nutrients from all plant life around it and left a path of decay wheresoever it walked. Black knight and grim steed were the very vision of apocalyptic portend, and as they neared the community, those in slumber took to fitful dreaming. Those who did not felt a sense of dread, the likes of which they'd never endured, and made a hurried lockdown of their homesteads. The clack of hooves on cobblestones was a morbid sound that spread the wraith of fear like an airborne contagion. An icy wind swept through in tandem, bringing yet more drifts to a place already in the grip of winter's fury.

In the square, beyond the hanging corpse at the gallows, the rider brought the phantom gelding to a standstill and reached inside a heavy, hooded robe. A doeskin purse contained two things. First produced was a fist-sized rock which was tipped into the mouth of the communal well to break the ice which had formed within. Before its descent into the water, the baron's heart, now riddled with writhing grubs, was examined for the last time and pitched into the town's supply. The deed was done, and so the push for the castle was the final leg of the journey.

In the last hour before dawn, guards were presented with another unearthly apparition in the wake of the ill-fated feast. Encircled and kept at distance by many a sentry's halberd, the hellish transgressor waited patiently as word of his arrival was sent to the new baron. In light of recent incursions by northern forces, and having been woken at an ungodly hour, the lord's response to the news was less than considered. Initially ordering melee, his command was rescinded on counsel from the matriarch.

There was much distrust of the pale man-at-arms among the household and its liegemen, save the former baroness who saw him as a necessary evil in a time of pending conflict with an emboldened enemy. She pushed for his presence at strategy meetings but was met with fierce resistance in the early days of engagement. Only when, for the third time in succession, the defending army had suffered heavy losses and had been forced to retreat once more, had the lord of the vale and his commanders relented. With the ground gained thus far, the invaders would soon be encamped on the outskirts of the vale, and, spurred on by minor victories, they'd push for one final assault to crush the opposition. It was posed by the vale's new advisor that their forces should set a trap for the northmen. Supply wagons should be abandoned, and small groups of men should take off in many directions to give an illusion of desertion, so that outriders would report of a faltering opposition. This tactic would prove the final enticement for an overly confident aggressor, and their leader should be left for him to deal with.

Without any plan to counter this, the defenders took their lead from the crone's eldritch warrior and sent instruction to the rank and file at the front line.

By nightfall of the second day thereafter, the invaders were encamped at the edge of the great forest and within striking distance of the hinterland's stronghold. With a watch set, they broke open barrels of ale and celebrated the sure victory to come. An old road through a dreary fen would carry man, horse, and provisions towards those fortifications at the break of day. Under the cover of the necromancer's sorcery, half of the defending army moved through the forest to outflank the enemy by taking up position at their rear. And through withering veins of woodland, the pale man-at-arms guided his deathly mount to the edge of cover and sought out the mind of the northern king. That night, the king's dream was one of unparalleled supremacy. He'd rise from slumber in his war tent to lead his army to the most brutal devastation of his reign so far. The valemen would be nothing more than a memory, come dawn.

The fen was an ancient sprawl of wet ground fed by cascading water which came down the tree-lined slopes and settled into the forest swamp. Its air was misery. Long dead was its story and the things it contained. And now, on this day of days, it was host to a war pack bent on destruction. They filed along its central track as a rumbling colossus. Banners of skull and bone held black flags which snaked on a breeze, and heavy armour gave rhythmic rattle to the death-dealers it encased. The crone had watched their progress from a hidden vantage since first light and knew the bait had been taken with blind ambition. These wetlands cradled her history and every wept tear of it had found its way symbolically into this dismal trough. All of it had cause to, as it was a build to this day and the further ruin it would be instrumental to. She moved position and turned her attention to giving a signal to the valemen who'd used her enchantment for cover. Emerging from the forest, they began a steady march through the northmen's abandoned camp toward the wetland gap.

South of the marshes, the young baron and the other half of his forces lay in wait for the first sign of the approaching host. Those who were his allies in this, the crone and her strange fighter, were elsewhere, and so his trust was entangled in the web of their machinations. All he could do was hold to hope and pray his alliance with the witch of root and earth didn't come to bear a rotten fruit. His outriders brought word that the enemy was on the move, and the push to engage on the fen road got under way. Taking his own solitary path, the architect of the stratagem guided his lifeless horse into the same drowned arena away from any and all. A sixth sense would hand him knowledge of all movement within the sunken space and aid his intent to single out the 'head of the serpent'. Mist pockets drifted over moss, pool, and skeletal tree and coated reed fronds the same in a slick of uncanny atmosphere. They brought eerie weather to a forlorn site and laid their blanket of sleep upon what would be the deathbed of many.

In the township, a curious malady had stricken the populace. Young and old alike had taken to their beds in the grip of a callous fever, bearing evil welts upon their bodies. Most thought it plague, yet either way there was no cure for the unknown agent among them. The corruption of the former baron's heart, enhanced by the application of a septic spellcasting, had brought the inhabitants to ruin in simple fashion. The water they'd drunk and then consumed in earnest in their attempts to quell the fire of a raging infection had imparted only an inevitable passing.

Infected households were daubed with the mark of the black dahlia, meaning death valley, and those therein were left to perish in isolation. None evaded its vile tendrils, with those tending to the sick and dying eventually succumbing to its stealthy infiltration of a defenceless community. Only those at the castle, with its separate water source, escaped the pestilence's insidious reach.

Each blighted dwelling was put to flame when all inside were taken by disease. Only the homes of the last left standing went unburnt, with no one there to complete the grim task. Instead of ash they became foul rot, and the air of the ghost town bore the stink of it. A place which had stood and thrived for more than two centuries now slipped into the clutches of a terminal decline. Never again would the market come to town. Not ever would seasonal festivities occur. And the sounds of children playing in its streets were buried in the ashes that littered those same empty lanes. A sinister quiet descended on the place and its hostility kept wildlife from its walls. Nothing remained except a lone raven, which toured the skyline and surveyed the wreckage of a long overdue retribution. After several passes, it veered away and returned to the evergreen of the great forest to descend and come to perch on the crone's left shoulder. In this way, she learnt the outcome of her malediction and revelled in the knowledge of its execution.

Looking one last time that morning into the scrying pool, she watched the northmen advance along the old fen trail and saw that all was as it should be. Their broad, timber wagons were drawn single file by heavy horse and divided down the line by marching men.

They outnumbered the valemen two to one, but with a lust for warfare that made it three by sheer intent. Many lands had fallen under the raging steel of this barbarian horde, and the vale would be the last acquisition to a territory which stretched from the northern ice floes to the jagged, vaulted peaks of the eastern divide. Their chieftain would have the baron as a pet if he survived this day's violence; a humiliation more cutting than any tempered blade. Not yet in the heart of the fen, the advancing army came to an abrupt halt, as riders sensed unease in their horses. It never failed to alert them to danger and so was never dismissed offhand.

They scoured for the source of it but found nothing, and it was a thing which gnawed at their leader. Perplexed, he gave an order to proceed with caution, and the weaponized bane of nations rumbled on.

At the height of the winter sun, light began to wane from the sky as the northmen reached the very centre of the wetland. Again, their horses faltered as a creeping calm took hold of the place. Their flags dropped, as what little breeze there was stole out of the stagnant scene. Save the odd clank of armour or neigh of horse, the silence became a focus none could ignore. And then the chieftain's mount reared up and kicked at the air at first sight of the apparition which emerged from thorny foliage. His ride was a shade of the netherworld, and his plate steel protection the very model of the darkest, arid tundra scorpion. He towered over the average man, with his frame more powerful than any in the ranks of the invading force. It went unsaid, but every one of them doubted their individual chances against him. In a slow, deliberate pace, he guided Hell's gelding towards them before coming to a stop in a pool of water. Warriors watched fern and wort choke to empty shell around him and made silent asks of their gods in the moment.

There was a measure of time when nothing moved in the space between them. Though brief, it became the catalyst for something unearthly to come. First a ripple here and there on surface water, and then suction beneath to form black swirls within the cold grip of a sodden incubator. For an age, they'd lain in the shallows;

those slain in battle when these lands were overthrown decades before. In answer to a necromantic summoning, they stood again on lifeless legs and rose at the behest of their new commander. All bleak-white bone and rusted armour, this army of the dead came to attention on either side of the old fen road; a foe the likes of which the northern horde had never encountered. Arrow and spear would prove redundant, and even blade would be near useless. Blunt would be their weapons of choice, but the defiant roars which went up front and rear of their column begged a different answer entirely. The baron's forces had converged upon their position, and now they stood between the living and the dead.

Still air became a storm of arrows, with movement the means to live, and facing down the enemy the only reason to draw breath. Chaos took control of the combat as the chance for any strategy fell away. Beyond the exchanges of airborne death waves aimed solely at those who wore flesh, bows were ditched in favour of close-quarter arms, and opponents came crashing together. A swift lesson in sorcery was meted out to the northmen; for every deathless fighter they felled, they watched it reanimate from a disembodied state. Each one would take its share of their number, but none they could take of theirs. For the first time in their lengthy battle history, they were the ones on the backfoot. Already, the fenland sinks turned red, and the butchery was a loss of head, limb, and bowels on a burgeoning scale.

Amid the carnage, the pale man-at-arms levelled his sword at the northern king and threw down an invite of one-on-one destruction. Met with zeal and fervent fury, they charged mounted at one another and closed the distance between them.

In a collision of unbridled aggression, both horse and rider apiece came together in a clash which brought all four to the ground. The chieftain was the first to his feet, and as the steeds scattered amongst the surrounding melee, the crone's champion first knelt, then slowly stood to wrap fists round axe and sword and strike them together in fatal gesture. And then the circling of each other began. The howling din of furious combat surrounded them, yet it fell away from the senses as they studied the weak points of opposition armour and the prowess of its wearer. Not as protected as his opponent, the barbarian assumed a greater agility but had yet to test that theory.

Bearing broadsword and a heavy gauntlet with a forearm-mounted buckler, he employed a pared-down halberd with his unprotected arm. Breastplate, horned helm, and studded hide covered most of him, save exposed thighs on legs stood in shin-plated boots. A black hand with a palm-centred eye motif sat upon the broad spread of his chest plate, being the symbol of fear and domination which had trampled the retaliation of lesser enemies. Its visage had cowed most men, but then the vale's protector was both man and something else entirely.

Their first sweeps were a clatter of steel on steel, as each deftly read the intent of the other. The sky had blackened in the short time since first encounter, and it spoke of a fell day to chart the passing of countless souls. In two swift arcs, their swords came together and locked at the hilts, and as much as the northman pressed his weight against the other's strength, he was repelled but ducked sufficiently as the backhand swipe of his opponent's battle-axe made minor contact with his helm. It was clear who possessed the greater brawn, and so the seasoned barbarian had to rely on tactic alone. Stepping in again, he kicked water from a stagnant pool into the face of his opponent and brought the edges of halberd and sword into contact with plate mail in the split-second confusion. They made only scratches to material forged in arcana, and the wearer countered with a blistering lunge, which saw a point of the battle-axe blade lock the weapon behind the top half of the barbarian's buckler and tear it clean off as they separated. Torn away by sheer strength, it dropped into the swamp to leave only the remnants of a chainmail glove about his left hand.

Loss of the buckler stole away protection and served as another display of the taller fighter's primal power. But there were other ways to defend, and a crossing of weapons would serve equally well. The battle raged on around them, but they were oblivious to its many casualties, being hellbent on each other's downfall. A succession of lunges, parries, and ripostes followed which culminated in a dance of sparks as their blades slid apart. It marked the measure of their equal prowess in battle, though with each exchange that passed, the human combatant began to suffer from fatigue. Knowing this, the northern king made a choice to sacrifice defence in order to gain the opportunity of bringing his enemy down with him. That he should die at the hands of such a deadly foe would be legend enough if he made their deaths as one. With the decision made, he shifted tactics, and his moves became those of subtle invitation. He used his wilt in stamina as a lure and waited for the right moment in their clash.

After a handful of brutal arcs, which the chieftain parried yet felt the epic force of each blow shock through him, he saw his chance. With both weapons aimed at the tall warrior's exposed neck, he lunged in a lancing counterstrike, knowing full well he'd be impaled in the process. And yet the move evoked a whole other outcome. In a lightning reflex, the breastplate formed by folded legs shot open for those appendages to ensnare their victim. Hauled from his feet, the northman could do nothing as the strength in those extended limbs became a crushing vice which pinned his arms to his sides and caused his weapons to drop from flexing hands.

Raised face to face with his nemesis, he could only roar his last defiance, as the handsome features peeled back to reveal the jaws of the true thing within, which then buried its fangs into the throat of its captive. There came a frenzy of gushing blood and guttural screams before a sharp wrench of the body and a deeper bite into the neck separated the head from the rest of him.

In the heat of battle, not many in the northmen's ranks caught sight of their leader's demise. On they fought in vain against a foe which could not be bested, and against another which possessed the will to defend its realm. Only when the victor put the king's head on the shaft spike of his axe and held it aloft in triumph did they lose heart.

Despite a bold last stand, the overwhelming press of enemies on all sides brought about a ghastly slaughter, with a broken few able to scatter into cover and use the wilds to escape the rest of the carnage. Black sky and red earth framed the harrowing scene, and the wails of the cleaved and dying drifted on the misery of the dismal fen. It was done, and the crone's lethal protagonist turned his eye to the baron. His forces too had suffered heavy losses, but this victory would make that sacrifice another jewel in the history of the vale. Collecting his horse, the man-at-arms mounted and surveyed what remained of the homeland guard.

"This count of souls is our bargain met," whispered the crone.

The spectre in the cave mouth behind her tilted its head in apparent agreement.

"The rest are to be left for another purpose," she added.

Turning, and leaning on her stave, she locked the gaze of phantom eyes. For decades, she'd made her pacts with what she called the 'astral orphans'; those cast out in the purge which shadowed mankind's infancy.

Demonologist, necromancer, conjurer … the title mattered not. Mere words which could not begin to encompass that which she'd mastered. Sworn hate had propelled her dark disenchantment with the world of men, and her pursuit of a darker means with which to bury it.

This day had been long in the making, and the converging of many things she'd woven had come together in a righteous bloodletting. And still, it wasn't done. There were strands of the whole yet to be affixed, and the hour grew late for their making.

With idle gesture, she dismissed the astral entity in the shadows to give her attention to a hex of a different slaughter.

It would crown a vengeance which had festered in her blackened heart since the vale was last washed in a crimson catastrophe. When she had been young and all innocence had been torn away.

Chapter Four

It was a hushed household which stood behind the high walls of the castle. Every man and strong lad who'd been able to bear arms had marched off under the baron's flag to engage the northmen. The usual contingent of servants had also been decimated by the pox which had overrun the township. No guards stood at duty, and all means of entry were firmly latched and bolted. The matriarch, her daughter, and a handful of housemaids waited for news from the battlefield and busied themselves with pointless tasks to keep their minds from imagining the worst. Vials of poison sat at hand should that news be grim to steal all inside away from a harrowing sexual ordeal at the hands of the horde. Since her husband's passing, the elder lady of the house talked at length with her daughter concerning her father's adulterous history. The maiden had always known but never voiced it, deeming it above her station in the family hierarchy. In recent times, they'd spoken candidly of his numerous infidelities, with the subject of the deal with the crone coming to light.

She understood full well her mother's want for a reckoning and was intrigued by the bargain she'd made with the woodland walker. She'd often taken to her bed pondering the uses of such a spellcaster, and the possibilities an alliance of that ilk might bring for a future kingdom. With a guile inherited from her father, she used the lack of security at the castle to bring a horse from the stable and took the back road to the forest her mother had spoken of. She aimed to throw in her lot with the conjurer before any bargains which did not include her were agreed with her brother. She would have no rule of men governing her can and cannots, as her blood was as noble as any male heir's. Snowdrifts made the trail difficult to follow, and many times she took a wrong fork en route to the wilderness. Daylight thinned by the time she crossed the shallow river and slipped into the dense growth of the ancient forest. Beyond this line, she had no sense of where the crone could be found. With darkness creeping in, and with a will not to abandon her mission, she pressed on and held to chance for the desired outcome.

There were many tales of night terrors in these woods; most superstition, but some well-earned. Wolves roamed here, as did wildcats and bears, and those things attributed to the crone herself. As a child, she'd been tucked up by maids who had stolen chances to tell her stories of the forest's lamentable past. Accounts of those who had never left, alongside more gruesome retellings of age-old fables had kept her from slumber many a night.

And now here she was, grown and seeking out the source of a number of those yarns, as the sun slipped from the sky and plunged the vast, cold greenwood into bitter night.

Soon the light took its exit entirely, and so her mount was the only one equipped to see. For a spell, they drifted through the ink of darkness before enchanted moonlight set down a path for her to follow. The mare between her legs seemed led by an unknown draw, and only when a startling handclap produced a sudden flare of light did they both panic. Her horse reared up as the robed figure responsible for the wash of illumination set the unnatural flame down on a fractured, woody stem and left it to burn on magical fuel.

A whisper of calm from the crone brought the animal under control before she took hold of its bridle and rubbed its muzzle for good measure. In now near daylight, the noble rider got her first look at the legend of the realm. There was no surprise in the eyes of the necromancer, as if the arrival of her visitor had been a thing known all along. She saw the bloodline in the young woman's features and guessed the nature of this late traversal of her dominion. Guiding the horse by its headgear, she took the highborn damsel to the site where no saplings could grow.

There was a whispered calm here, and a lone, fractured bough of an age-old tree which had been dragged to the spot for some hidden purpose. That her father perished here in the clutches of a nightmarish mutation she knew not, and the crone would not venture that particular detail. Dismounting, the vale maiden put a boot on the very bough on which he'd been ripped apart and began her questioning of the author of his demise.

"My mother has spoken much of you. Of how you quelled her shame and put a protector among us in these dreadful times."

She of dark art scanned the unblemished skin and fine lines of her uninvited guest and ignored the statement.

"I was once very much like you. So young, unknowing, and full of dreams."

Her response hung as a wistful remembrance.

"But, as in all things, I learnt the true nature of what I was when wolven men brought their predatory ways into my fairy tale existence."

The maiden pulled her riding shawl tightly about her to counter the icy chill of winter's breath. She noted the crone appeared unaffected by what stung at her. Unsure as to why the witch seemed to ignore what she'd said and focused instead on her youthful appearance, she pressed for an answer on something.

"Is it true you've made a bargain with my brother?"

It pulled the elder from her musing, and she turned to look her in the eye.

"No pact have I made with your sibling heir. He rode to war on the echoes of your mother's request."

She cocked her head a little, inviting another query from her visitor, who'd been happy to learn no covenant had been agreed with her brother. "Then will you deal with me, as you did my mother?"

"To what end, child?"

She paused and recalled those thoughts she'd toyed with when formulating her own plan for the advancement of her family's fortunes. The crone merely stared back as this tasty morsel inched closer to ensnarement in a web she couldn't see.

"The women of this family are the rightful makers of our fate. My brother, like my father before him, is drunk on entitlement and on whatever he can exploit for personal gain."

The crone could only laugh.

"You talk as if I have no knowledge of these things. I need not your words to understand the hearts of men."

She turned away and waved a hand distractedly.

"You should go … and waste my time no longer."

More bait for the inexperienced.

"I've not sought you out to be dismissed so lightly," the maiden countered.

"That kind of steel will lead you down dark paths, lady fair. Be careful what you desire in this garden of good and evil."

It was a warning like all others given. A rightful pause for thought handed to any who brought their bargains to her table. Due caution met, she waited for what this lily of the vale would pitch.

"I wish no true ill upon my brother. But, if some future malady were to befall him and render him incapable of performing his duties for the kingdom, then someone would have to step from the shadows and take up the seat of power. If we are to avoid any undue instability."

How loveless this bloodline was, thought the crone. Like beasts of the wild they sometimes eat their own, and how they resembled her favoured eight-legged species.

"And what measure of sickness should afflict your lord?"

"Sufficient that he may no longer influence family affairs but not enough to ruin all reason to live."

"And, if I agree to this, what do you pledge to the coffers of the kings of chaos?"

"I do not understand. My bargain is with you and no other."

"A bargain with me is a pact with eternity and the ones who dwell in the shadows."

It was a gravity she'd not expected, but then again, an understanding of it all evaded her sphere of experience. Blinded by ambition and thrilled by an offered alliance with this legendary conjurer, she nodded acceptance.

"Then it is agreed," said the crone.

Moving to a sackcloth bag which had stood at the edge of the artificial light she'd created, the witch of root and earth reached in, and brought forth a small, wooden box.

"Take this to the castle. Never open it except on the day I send a raven as a sign. Inside lies your brother's undoing. The false flame I made on your arrival will follow you to the edge of the forest. Beyond that, you must find your own way back."

Flushed with success and cradling the box of tricks which contained her future, she rode her mare from the garden of good and evil and took another bargain beyond the walls of the castle.

The Art of Boxing Clever

The day of the great battle came and went, yet no word of the outcome had reached the ruling household. The matriarch's daughter had gone missing, but had returned in the early hours unscathed. It had been a time of great worry for the elder noblewoman, but now all that remained was to hear good news from the young baron's cohorts.

It came not the day after, or even the one beyond that. It wasn't uncommon for fighting men to encamp after conflict to tend to the wounded and build pyres for the dead. She assumed her son engaged in that very activity and quietly hoped it so. The fact the northmen had not breached the family stronghold gave her cause for a belief in a vale-won victory. Many times she'd considered the notion of sending a servant on the long hike to acquire information; even take a horse herself in pursuit of it.

But in time of war, she knew the lands could be crawling with splinters from the great horde, and so stayed her want for an answer. The halls of the castle were empty and still, and she longed to fill them with joy and laughter. In the vale maiden's bed chamber, the lid of a small, wooden box came slowly open. The forest dweller which had occupied the space inside crawled out and scuttled away into the shadows of a vaulted corner. In nooks and crannies, it kept to hidden ways within the grand expanse, finding a route to the cellars to begin its task. There, it birthed its offspring; a myriad of tiny simulacra which grew at speed in sorcery and populated the space beneath the near-empty household.

Spinners all, they began a dressing of the dark, damp space, and prepared a chamber full of goods to welcome a number of evils. The opened container, which had housed the spider, went unnoticed by the maiden, as she'd hidden it neath her bed lest servants stumble upon it. In this way, she had no knowledge of its unsealing, and hence no awareness of a bargain steeped in deceit. It wasn't long at all before the arachnids had woven an enormous construct of threads; a matrix of necromantic intent.

In the great forest, its warden prepared to leave the place which had been her home for over four decades. Many strands had been spun in that span of time which had led to this moment. A barb of fate had placed her there to begin with, so no rend of heart preceded the exit of it. All she owned would fit into one small sack, a thing to shoulder when no brief look back would be given. A final sortilege of bird bones on the fractured bough in the clearing where no saplings could grow told her the movements of her pale man-at-arms.

Satisfied, she gathered them up and set off on her last walk through a wilderness full of perils; ones far less deadly than those she administered. Her path became a passage accompanied by fanfare, as all wild things came to line the route and pay their respects to the one who had watched over them. Wolves howled a lament, while birds took to tree canopies and voiced their own addition to a sorrowful symphony. Many forms of blood and bone brought notes worthy of the warden's status. She projected her love of all of them, and the promise of a welcome to any who would venture inside the boundary of her new home.

Winter was in full grip, and the deep freeze breathed her icy intent over the vale. It sat at lower elevation before her, wrapped in a white shroud befitting its fall into disarray. It would take a day of walking to reach her destination; yet should she employ magic, it would be instant. However, the trek would give her time to ponder much in the way of doom and provide a last, long look at the arresting wilds. She headed to where she'd come from all those years ago in a time of desperate calamity.

War had severed a connection to the human realm and put her at the mercy of the badlands, and now she was righting that historic wrong. Orphaned to inhospitable terrain, she'd stumbled upon the hermit who'd given her shelter to then become a student in the game of survival. Adept at all he taught, she surpassed his capabilities and set her heart on a long scheme of rightful resurgence. At its ending, the time spent in the pursuit of it would have no meaning, and she would bask in the renewal of the outcome. Alas, the true perpetrator would pay not, but his lineage would answer for the crime in his absence.

Beneath the ground, in the dank castle cellars, the spinneret strands of an insect workforce hung ready for their intended purpose. A vast, three-dimensional ball of silk hung in the vaulted store, bearing a dim glow which did nothing to lift the cold of the place. It hummed with the energy of spellcraft, as the primer for something else to occur. After hours in static suspension, it began to pulse and vibrate on the charge it contained. Woven symbols sitting in the outer threads, which kept it anchored to wall and beam, flared their own additions of light in an augmenting sequence. A howl, low level at first, writhed free of its centre. Its tone was insidious, and it altered in pitch as it grew in volume. Strange shadows began to creep across walls and ceiling as the inner space of what was, in essence, a sizeable summoning circle opened a gate between worlds.

And the spill of things which followed was truly of horror. They crept on contorted limbs from a rend in the fabric of reality to a household which would be host to their terror. The witch's astral orphans had sent their minions through, and these lesser devils were to be the haunt of a place which would know her wrath. They gathered in a warren now turning back to gloom, as the glare of crafted light burned low. Entities of sinister design and at one with the shadows, they used that dark material to slip into the inner workings of the castle and begin the ills of their instruction.

In stone and stout rafter, they coiled throughout, taking woe and mayhem with them. The ancient site groaned a whisper with their passing, as they stripped bad memories from its structure so those small evils could feed their greater own. To find the living of this edifice was their goal, and to bring them fear and loathing the rest of it. Their presence here was determined by a necromantic hourglass; though unseen, it brought just enough movement of sand to the endgame.

A bad feeling was only the beginning for those women entrenched within the stronghold. A chill of more than what a season could bring snaked all around them. Even in chambers warmed by open fires could they see their breath. With extra layers donned, they went about their duties complaining that this winter was the worst in living memory. Including matriarch and daughter, nineteen warm bodies moved through this plunge in temperature and were already succumbing to the mal-intent of it. Small flames atop candles flickered as fell haunters swept passed them. It was noticed by a number, who dismissed the occurrences as draughts come in on the thrust of venomous gales. In the scullery, washing water turned stagnant in its trough before a layer of black ice came to crown its surface. Wherever the liquid sat within the castle, it did the same by the time the many visitations were complete. But yet again, upon discovery, such phenomena they attributed to a brutal onslaught of weather. And so began the individual torment of each highborn and servant alike.

In her private quarters, the vale maiden moved closer to the stoked-up fire on the hearthstone and pulled a blanket around her shoulders. She shivered despite these measures, and then jumped in her chair as all candles save one in the room snuffed out. Something primal told her a presence was near, and an odour so vile confirmed it. After her meeting with the crone, the truth of things supernatural seemed very real to her, and so she doubted it not. Still, caution and fear welled up in equal measure, and she reached for kindling to take flame from the fire and relight the gutted candles. Her movements were focused and deliberate in an attempt to stave off the panic which would have her take flight from the room. With tongue of flame now acquired, she tentatively stood and set about bringing more illumination back to a chamber darkened by the onset of evening. With each light source relit, she felt a minor hike in her confidence until the fourth rekindled cast a glow which defined the features of a horrifying grotesquery.

It reached out with foul limb, and she screamed the enticement it wanted to hear. Like a dread, rotting hybrid of canine and insect, it arched its abdomen from the floor and hissed at the mortal to be gone in an instant when she made for the door. It scuttled up vertical stone and seemed to merge with the shade of a timber ceiling. Whether it had departed or not she cared little, for she intended no return, and instead ran screaming for the attention of any who might hear.

A creeping hoarfrost engulfed the passageway she stepped into, and she slipped on the crisp covering to fall headlong into a space which was having the torches in its wall sconces extinguished in quick succession by an unseen agent. Soon, she'd have to flee its entire length in the dark and had no intention of returning to her quarters for a candle. With a little light remaining at the far end, she got up and struggled to make headway fast with the freeze underfoot. By the time she got just halfway down the corridor, icy air sucked out the last of the torch fires and plunged the whole stretch of it into darkness.

In the great hall, a handful of subordinates put the finishing touches to tables set out for a celebratory feast ordered by the matriarch to buoy spirits, as in her mind it was another way of drowning thoughts of a battlefield defeat. Though busied, each of them was cold to the core, as an eerie chill laid a crystallised mantle over floor, tables, and the dining ware they laid in place. Rafter-hung tapestries froze rigid, and what open flames there were simply died in the cradles they sat in.

Stopped in their tracks, the servants tried to focus on one another in the near dark, with only moonlight streaming in from tall windows. All heard a distant, muffled scream as what fall of natural light came in seemed to twist into the most malevolent of shapes. A foul stench accompanied the unearthly movements, and noises so faint in tandem could be heard. They felt the surrounding of terrors and found each other by accident in the centre of the space, having been corralled there by an unseen threat.

Being the last to feel the cold burn of an unnatural biting freeze, the matriarch, ensconced within the war room, looked up from a map of the realm spread out upon the tabletop and knew death's reach had come a-calling. Maternal instinct and decades of experience served her well.

Even before the frost and creeping cold had entirely enveloped that wing of the castle, she'd sensed an ominous menace looming beyond the threshold. As that spread of dreadful suspension advanced, she understood a pact made long ago was levying its toll for the execution of it. Her time had run out, and the wyrd wolves at the door were here for the deathwatch. She sensed their movement before any sighting of them, with their subtle noises bleaching through in the switch between corporeal and non-corporeal phases. In this way, they passed through solid substance to then materialise on the other side. Room timbers groaned in a grip of the freeze, and as frost bloomed like icy spores, it took her breath as ingredient and left her lungs strained as a nightmare entered the chamber.

All embers went dead. She smelt its malodour, but saw it not. When it passed by the windows of the south face, she caught a glimpse of its outline and shuddered. Instinct made her crouch low and move to a corner, but her body heat was red radiance to a thing with eyes for tracking. Whimpering and bringing arms and legs close, she sat at the farthest point she could and prayed for a swift end. Its drool, and the toxin it contained, dripped from a maw housing black molars and incisors and extended red canines. In the freeze that drool froze not, being spatters instead on a crystalline carpet. Eyes of gloss grey and flesh of rotted waste, its walk resembled insectoid but its hunting said wolfish. Coming closer, it sampled the air, and the sound made her wince. Each step it took put an ache in her bones, and she thought she might die from the horror of it. A foul exhalation wrapped about her, with the absence of light saving the sight of an extending set of jaws, which opened after into a halo of death over her head. Its saliva fell and coated her skin, but was pulled back in by the coiling tongue which slowly licked the face of its cornered quarry.

Each space of the family fortress saw a sample of this wintry visitation when at last every dimension of it was delivered into darkness. Household minions filled the new empty with their screams wherever lich-lycans found and tormented them. By design and casual menace, their foes drove them from all sites to have them assemble in terror in the great hall, joining those already there for a greater torment to come. With a few handheld torches relit, they formed a crude circle at the heart of the hall and tried to calm one another in what seemed the hour of their doom. Matriarch and daughter acted no better than the rest in the face of an end by unhallowed means. The hell shapes harried them, shifting in and out of phase to appear amongst their group, which sent the women scattering in all directions to just simply encounter others doing the same. Their screams were a banquet for things which dined on fear, and on an endless supply they gorged themselves. Wrapping tongues round ankles, they upended targets and dragged them away into the shadows before letting go to leave them stranded from the rest. It was a morbid entertainment which went on all night.

Only when a thin, grey sunrise put its first shaft of light through a window did they relent. Drained of hope, tears, and utterly exhausted, the women saw respite for the first time as their terrorizers began to slowly inch away. The bitter cold remained in residence, as daylight's arrival merely forced retreat, not exit. They became the stuff of gossamer once again and went into the walls. Though dawn seemed a salvation, the haunting continued, as every move was shadowed by invisible fiends bent on keeping their captives herded. Attempts at escape were thwarted at every turn, and despair became as chilling as the reach of these evil guardians. It was a soul-destroying scenario, in the very sense of it, and its proponents grew strong while their victims diminished. Unrelenting, the day's hours crawled by, and never far from the great hall had they gotten before being pushed back through a maze of misery. But their spirits soared at the sound of the portcullis being heft mid-afternoon. Surely, the menfolk had returned, and the horror would be driven from the workings of the stronghold.

All a servant could see from her vantage was a lone rider carrying the fluttering standard of the noble household and bearing a sackcloth bag. A brief glimpse was all she got, but enough to tell her they had something to cling to. Informing the others, they groaned collective relief, and held that thought to see them through until rescue. Before long, the clink of plate armour could be heard beyond the main door, and not too much thereafter came the sound of its unlatching. It swung open with a sense which seemed to banish the frost and murk within, as the pale man-at-arms stood bearing the colours of the bloodline in one hand and the head of the one he'd slain in battle in the other. Many fell to their knees as the moment proved too much. The matriarch ran forward in joy, only to slow, then falter in step as the warrior threw the head at her feet. It rolled to a stop and stared in lifeless gaze at the source from whence it came. And then she too came to her knees.

With the battle won, the crone's champion had turned his attention to the young baron. The undead army, unstoppable and unrelenting, had been pitched against the hinterland force, and so made the fenland trail a corpse road for the men of both sides. Her flesh and blood had been butchered, and this horrid token of what was left signalled the death of her household. The door slammed shut and locked behind the warrior, and the flag he bore clattered to the floor. Outside, the crone crossed the courtyard cobbles and then flew apart in an upward swirl of cawing ravens, only to rematerialise at the fighter's side and look upon vale ladies with menace. It was a moment more dreadful than any of the long night they'd endured. As disaster loomed, the baron's sister, who'd sought to betray him, realised the betrayal which she herself had suffered. In bitter anger, she stepped forth and screamed her defiance at the witch of root and earth and demanded that her bargain be bound and true. It brought a cackle more sinister than lich-lycan stealth, but the crone entertained her nonetheless.

"And which part of our bargain have I broken, sweet little child?"

"All of it … in every way. I am owed the fulfilment of our pact."

The crone raised a finger and wagged it slowly.

"Ah … but you see, my dear, I have honoured exactly what you asked. Your words were thus: 'someone would have to step from the shadows and take up the seat of power'. Well, my little darling … that someone has arrived."

Chapter Five

The man-at-arms unsheathed his sword and withdrew the battle-axe from its binding. His handsome features peeled back to reveal the jaws of the true thing within. There'd been screams before, but they paled in comparison to those uttered in the face of death. Nineteen warm bodies were about to go cold in the most brutal way possible. He advanced and they scattered, but it was only the beginning. It was a scene the crone had waited nearly five decades for, and she relished every bloody cleave of it. The first of them was rent in two as a side swipe sent her upper half sailing into a pack of fleeing others. Her innards fell clear of the torso, and the slick caused others to fall. While down, one received an axe blow which split her head clean down the middle and caused the blade to lodge in the spine before he tore it free. Another was decapitated by his other hand in the same move, as sword found tender neck. Amid the unfolding carnage, the matriarch remained kneeling in shock before the one who'd come to depose her.

Blood was already pooling from the rending of three as he gave chase to the remainder. Desperate, some raced to windows and tried to hurl themselves through thick forest glass panes. They merely cracked or shattered causing those attempting escape to be momentarily stunned and easy prey in the process. Three of the four he dispatched with ease, while one scrambled away during their demise. A pair of them went by blow of sword and axe apiece, while the last of the trio took the bite of both weapons square in the shoulder blades. By now, the vale maiden was hysterical and screaming for this madness to stop. Hideous for the many, but delicious for the one, as the witch of root and earth stood a euphoric voyeur. Taking time to drag corpses to the centre of the chamber, the fighter ensured their greater expulsion of blood was kept to a designated spot as their bodies bled out. On he raged, swift in the chase and savage in the kill. He ignored matriarch and daughter, keeping his intent on their entourage. Six were diced and draining, and the rest were wailing along with crone laughter in the chamber. The necromancer mused this wasn't the first time she'd brought entertainment to this hall.

The next to perish was spliced from chin to navel, as one of the two-foot-long blades of the double-headed axe embedded in the cornered girl. Punched clean through her, the steel chimed off the stonework behind. He spun, and the motion propelled her body from the weapon for it to slide across the floor and crumple against the growing pile of others.

In feeble moves, some picked up chairs and bowls from the banquet tables and weakly tried to repel him. Such things either broke against his armour or from the blows he dealt them. By now, the vale maiden had dragged her mother to her feet, and together they ran to the doors and beat in vain against their timbers. All of these acts were sublime, and made the crone drunk on the grimdark of it all.

A further four were dispatched on the tables they tried to clamber over. Limbs fell away in quick succession as a blistering assault reduced them in a frenzy of screams and butchery. It was a burgeoning bloodbath, and once again he made sure the remains found their way to the central stack.

Only six terrified servants remained. He'd made short work of the others and thought it time to play a little. A severed arm made a quick meal, as he crunched through bone like butter and wore its red wash all over his monster maw. It heightened horror in the last of them before he set about the next wave of annihilation. Tossing the weapons aside, he assumed his full form with tucked legs unfurling and a drop down on all limbs. A dreadful head reared up and hissed at the meat before powering at fell speed into the group of them. Serrated armour did the work of discarded blades, and vile mandibles the rest, as he danced over and amongst them. It was a spurting, crimson finale in what had been a rampage beyond reason. They disassembled in pairs, and the gore was a litter he kicked around in his passing. When the bloodlust subsided, he was covered in a patchwork of viscera and had to shake the pieces off in the gathering up of the mess. The flesh and bone jigsaw was dumped with the other pieces, and it was time to deal with the highborn.

There were no words from the crone or her enforcer. No ceremony for something which had been long in the making. She simply looked their way and he obliged. The final act would have the matriarch witness the ending of her daughter before she too passed from this world. He made the prowl slow and deliberate, another stalking on top of the many she'd endured the night through. Her mother put herself between them, but the flick of a limb sent her spinning. Against the wall, the maiden could go no further, and then by the throat she was hoisted and pulled near. Dead eyes levelled inches from hers, as limbs snaked around to pin the rest of her. A frail scream faltered in her mother as one hand covered the maiden's face and the other took hold of her lower jaw. There was a gagging sound, followed by a full shudder of the body … followed by a crack like breaking pottery … and then a rasping tear which saw jawline and throat come away from head and torso. A fountain of blood gushed from the body which was tossed with the rest. Her mother's fate was the same, and when it was done, the crone gazed at her reflection in the hall's red pool and smiled a crooked smile. Distracted, her man-at-arms chewed the flesh from each jawbone and began a fashioning of sorts from both pieces.

A Long Time Ago

A time of peace and tranquillity came to an abrupt, horrid end. The vale was plunged into war in the final days of summer. Its seat of power was under siege from a usurper who was bent on expanding his domain. Like a choking, black cloud, his army appeared on the horizon and purged all valleys before it in the last push for the stronghold. Fleeing refugees brought word of a terrible enemy, with stories of torture, impalement, and the burning of all villages and holy sites. It was told the monks of an abbey were all beheaded, with said heads being fed to the army's hunting dogs. At the castle, the ruling family made their preparations for the coming wrest of their kingdom. The baron instructed guards to ensure the escape of his loved ones should the fortress fall into foreign hands. They were to be ushered out through the secret passage, which ran beneath the courtyard, and ferried away to safety. He himself would lead his forces against the invader and retreat to defend the walls if they were pushed back from the battlefield.

But there were snakes in his entourage. Promises of land and title proved irresistible to those who'd made pacts with the coming deathdealers. In their betrayal, the homeland army was ambushed on the fen road and slaughtered in the deadly crossfire from hidden archers and crossbowmen. The last brave souls, including the baron, fought hand-to-hand with a surrounding force and joined the rest of their number in a watery grave. When word of defeat reached the castle, knives were drawn, and his kin were put to death. In the moment of ruin, a daughter took flight and fled the fort by other means.

When the usurper learnt of her escape, he ordered same dogs which had feasted on ecclesiastical flesh be loosed to bring her down. Given scent from clothing, they pursued and led handlers to the river which skirted the great forest. That she'd crossed was obvious, and so they did the same and picked up her trail on the other side. The evergreen cover meant nothing to a pack which tracked her by smell, and her stamina would be waning with each step.

Near spent, she heard the sounds of her canine pursuers grow ever louder as she spilled from dense foliage to a site where no saplings could grow. There was a whispered calm here, and a lone, fractured bough of an age-old tree which had been dragged to the spot for some hidden purpose. She knew it would end here, in some way, and gave herself to the moment in this timeless place. The dogs burst clear of cover ... *it mattered not*. Their handlers kept them reined and drew weapons ... *so be it*. And then the terror came as the wide, blue sky faded from sight. She came to with a figure leaning over her. He held out a hand, which she took and was then standing. The day was still beautiful, but an acrid smell lent a hint of the unpleasant to it. He said but one thing, then turned and would have her follow.

"Who are you that walks among the graves of giants on this … fated hour?"

Hounds and handlers lay all about her. Charred to ash and separating slowly on a summer's breeze. The stranger was old and had gnarled stave to hand to support a frame which wore the meagre robe of a wild-home hermit. He waited not for her company, but assumed she'd follow. After all, she was now an orphan and dispossessed of these lands. She did indeed follow, to caves in the mountainside, and in her heart, she knew this would become her new home. Never could she return to the vale. Those who had betrayed her father would know her face, and her throat would meet steel in an instant. There was nothing but to begin again in this wildfell place. In time, she came to understand the nature of the man who had come to her aid. He cared not for the empty ambitions of other men and had walked from their world long ago. Here, in the palace of nature, he'd become as one with forces which had hewn the Earth from fire and chaos. They were his to command, and he wielded the power of the storm, the energy of the water, and the might of sun and moon.

These things she would learn, but dark was her heart, and so darker became her art. Her path to sorcery was a necromantic branch, and it reached into those facets of nature concerned with shadow and scare. As she advanced, her teacher grew older, and one day was gone when his time of flesh was spent. Alone, she made allies of wolf, raven, and other forest denizens and dealt on occasion with whatever fools chose to seek her out. In the pitch black of the mountain haunt, she harboured hatred of those who'd brought scars to her lineage and left her bereft of a place in the world of men. As the years were consumed, and her beauty waned, she lost too, the chance of mortal fulfilment and offspring. The usurper, aged too and in failing health, was succeeded by his eldest son so that the injustice would go on indefinitely. Like his father, he believed his noble right to whatever he desired was his entitlement. And so the vale lands of yore, under a rightful banner of ownership, became nothing more than a distant memory. In the shadows, in the heart of the great forest, the most powerful conjurer there'd ever come to be vowed a reckoning before her life was done.

Chapter Six

Her past had destroyed her. So much taken away in so few hours. The reflection in the blood pool was of someone she did not recognise. A number of suitors had courted her, and there'd been plans of marriage to the one she'd given her heart to before her hopes and dreams had been trampled by the dark ambitions of others. What was broken could never be fully remade, but she would have some of it returned by will and witchcraft in the hall where she'd dined and danced often back then. Getting slowly down on all fours, the crone put her hands into the slick, and got lower so she could sample it. Lick followed lick, and then incantation whispers which began to push smaller pools and rivulets towards the main body of the spill. With bloody mouth and hand, she wove her doll of dire making.

From pulses first it rose, taking form as she breathed arcane encouragement for growth. It evolved as it did in twisting streams that brought guise into its make-up. Taking shape as a womanly figure, it finally came upright in a crimson-death copy of her former self. Removing her black fabric of cover, she stood bare and stepped into the construct of blood. It covered every inch of her and rippled with hidden purpose, as the first of the spiders from the cellars crept into the hall. The man-at-arms backed away, allowing access to her on all sides. And so began another silken sleeve for change. They crept in hundreds over her and brought their wrappings to the whole which became suspended from pillar and rafter. When done, the chrysalis hung above the floor and heaved on the squirms within. Her enforcer continued his crafting of the jawbones and waited for what was to come. It was only hours in the making, and in the process, the cocoon's translucent wall revealed a thrash of limbs which moved through an egg-white liquid and brought her face, on occasion, to the surface. The crone was in the grip of an altogether strange transformation: one of shadow and scare.

As day began a fall away to dusk, activity in the chrysalis grew still. It no longer throbbed with vital energy, but merely vibrated every now and then in eerie ways. Threads as thick as stout cord kept the sack a good measure from the floor. Beneath, the corpses which had given up blood for the ritual were a pale white sculptured artwork on a congealed carpet. As the last ray of light dipped below the horizon, and when darkness stole in to claim the dead as its own, a single fingernail pierced the cocoon wall from within, and the pus of suspension began a slow spill. The first of it was foul spatters, followed by a steady pour which dripped onto the floor to form yet another pool beneath. The prelude to a dramatic emergence, it was slight in comparison to that which followed. From a full rupture, she came cascading down. Reborn unto this world, she seemed a hybrid of youth and old age. Perfect skin and voluptuous figure were in contrast to yellowed teeth, greyed hair, and lacklustre nails. She lay motionless, as the first of it was endured and over.

But in her art there was no outcome without there first being pain. As the next wave of it hit, her back arched and all limbs flexed to contractions which came to shudders. She loosed a howl like nothing other in the world and went to spasm as the rest of it inched out. Brand new teeth began the push from behind the old. All in her head were subjected to the pressure and were punched out of their sockets in a replenishment that came all at once. Her own blood followed rattles of enamel on stone, as the shed dental ware dropped all around her. So too were nails replaced all at once on hands and feet. It was a torture born of the price that had to be paid; slow and excruciating on purpose, being contractual with dark forces as it was. When finally the agony subsided, she lay still and wept with the joy of renewal, as the result came to fruition with the loss of silver hair and a rapid regrowth of youthful, golden strands.

The man-at-arms pulled a tapestry down from a rafter and wrapped her reborn form in it. Into sleep she slipped and was carried to a bedchamber for rest. Weakened by rejuvenation, she kept to slumber for days. In that time, he cleared the pile of gore from the great hall and stripped the household of trinkets honouring a bloodline which had deposed her own. Of the flesh gathered, certain things he kept, as per prior instruction, and burnt the rest on a bonfire in the grounds. When finally she woke, the castle was itself reborn and ready for a new era under her dominion. Fine clothing and jewellery she donned again; all things to frame fierce beauty. The hour of her ascendance was at hand, and she swept from private quarter to the room where all of great import took place. A good many had come to witness this investiture, but few in number were human. Only those who'd helped shape the path of her destiny were bestowed the great honour of invitation. And so the gypsies stood among the creatures of the wilds and bowed low.

In the chair of knotted oak and steel, the one her father had commanded of craftsmen, she took her rightful place in a hall visited by wolves, ravens, and other denizens of the forest. A coronet fashioned from the jawbones of those she'd brought low was placed upon her head by her enforcer. Some would say a queen of death, but in her mind she was simply the lady of the vale at last. A trove of gifts was bestowed, and slight though they were, they meant more to her than all the riches of the world. Bones there came from wolf, along with moss and fern from those of wing, and river-worn pebbles from the mouths of others. Nature's gem, gold, and silver for a monarch of a majestic wilderness. And a pendant, coveted by wildfolk, was presented and put about her neck so it would sit over the heart and shield it ever again from harm. There was no feast, nor fanfare, for she now wished her parlour emptied, and she'd spend the remains of the day on a wander of her home.

Many were the rooms which brought back fond memory, but none more so than where, as a child, she'd played. Grand it was not, being simple and plain, but had been a canvas she'd covered in her imagination. Here, there'd been daydreams of ruling the kingdom, and too it was the place where her mother had told her fairy tales of the spiderfolk who lived in the great forest. *What better place to make her new wants and wishes come to life?* Summoned, the man-at-arms brought the things she requested and so began the last chapter in a chronicle of the uncanny. Ripped out, the baron's head and spine had been kept and brought, along with her meagre possessions, in a sack she'd carried from the forest. Hacked clean off, his son's the same, was another of the things she'd asked be spared of burning. And to make those family trophies complete, the mutilated remains of matriarch and maiden fair were deposited also.

Of corpse and lifeless ruin, these pieces were administered surgical demonology, in itself a spell of necromantic cutting. The parts unneeded, the limbs of the baroness and daughter, were removed and fed to the man-at-arms. They were the offerings given in exchange for 'other pieces of arachnid origin' which were grafted to reimagined corporal shards. Effigies of root, twine, and dark ochre were fashioned with great care and then set to flame with the smoke blown by mouth over the motionless constructs. As the hexen dollies reduced, the incantation was evoked between creeping fumes which slipped in eldritch ways into the nose and throat of each. And so it came to pass in the most empty hour of the night, that new life was born from the entrails of death, and their cries were another weeping of the walls. There was a whole other lifetime to live within this great abode, and company would be needed for that span. They would be her playthings and would do all at her behest until that time expired. Part human, part something else, they were the spiderfolk of memory made manifest, as all those she'd made in her quest for vengeance. She had them know who they were and what they'd become, so that their suffering would be enduring to the end.

A Fairy Tale Ending?

There were those who wanted not her ascendency. They'd answered her call when there was nothing but despair and emptiness. Through them, she'd filled the void in her life and now, complete again, she needed them not. The alliance had brought the astral orphans numerous souls over the decades, and they were loath to relinquish such an arrangement. Where once they were conjured regularly, rare was the occasion she gave them a bridge unto this world. In those few chances, they'd seize the opportunity to bring their guile to bear upon her new-found solitude. Each commune was a way to seek advantage, and they would drag her soul to Hell if one slip she made. Always, they sought a reacquaintance with the old ways, but she would not yield to their black requests. And so this impasse crept on down the years to become a most hated deadlock between themselves and this defiant mortal.

Five winters on, in a fleeting moment where her guard was down, they saw what truly lay in her heart and discovered the chink in her armour. Winter storms in the region were the stuff of legend, but none so like the one which descended that year. Not often did travellers take a route through the vale, for its grim history made most keep to other roads. But a bitter afternoon swept a lonesome wayfarer to the castle gate, and near to death he was found by her enforcer. Carried to a bed chamber, a fire was lit, and the stranger was given slow revival in the cradle of her welcome. He was handsome and strong, but had a boyish charm which made her catch her breath when they talked. Taking her leave and retiring that evening, she thought of nothing save he until sleep finally took her. Another grim season now seemed the brighter, as she would have him stay, at the very least, until the thaw came and made the vale roads passable again. In old age, seclusion had been a comfort. Now rejuvenated, it was a curse. His coming here had wakened a want she'd not felt since the time of her betrothal, and for all of her control she was powerless in the pull of it.

"Tell me, what places of this world have you seen on your travels?"

They sat by the fire in the great hall and dined at a small table for an intimate air as she posed her question. She'd put her spiderfolk minions in suspension in the cellars lest their outlandish form be fright enough to have him flee. Instead, in need of servants, she'd sent a raven to the wildfolk, and they would be of service for as long as required.

"I have crossed the great peaks that touch the sky in the east. Locked in ice, those vast rocks are like the backbone of the world. So too, the endless burning sands of arid countries have known my footprints. Many lands in-between I have seen, and yet none can match the beauty of the one who now gives me shelter."

His words were sustenance. They brought exotic imaginings but were also the simple act of a man clearly infatuated with her, which was something all the sorcery in the world could not make real.

"Your bearing and way with words tell me you are no commoner. Where are you from, and what birthright do you hold?"

Tall, dark, and handsome, he was everything she desired with her body, and the mysteries of his mind and background were intoxicating.

"Where the land meets the great ocean to the west, my family holds sway over a sprawling kingdom. Prince is my title, but in myself I know only a man whose heart was made for adventure."

In the moments their eyes met, she felt life was full of endless possibilities, and merely in his company alone, the fires of passion went unchecked in her blood. To a wielder of such power, and one who'd known many horrors, these small things of everyday life scared her the most.

His presence seemed to bring a dispelling of winter. Soon, the thaw came, but neither one had any intention that he be on his way. The corridors and chambers were filled with warmth and laughter, all of which she'd wanted before cruel fate had torn them away so very long ago. With the hinterland now free of snow and frost, they took many rides into the wilderness. Of course, she knew every inch of it, and he was given tours of the great forest, its caves, and everywhere else within her borders. In the coming of spring, they'd take off together on small adventures where they'd make a shelter, a fire, and sleep under the stars. She'd told him much of her history, but had left out all the damning detail, and, to his surprise, he found her adept at a number of things such as fishing, food foraging, and building with nature's materials. Eventually, they could keep their flesh apart no longer, and in truth, she'd been a virgin until that moment. It was everything she'd imagined it would be, and it fulfilled a desire she'd turned into her broiling vengeance a whole other lifetime ago.

She was now free to enjoy what had died in the fires of war and betrayal. It wrapped her up and consumed her, and she let it flow wild through her being. And the thing which would make it all complete came unto her. Before summer, she was with child, and her heart was filled with what she'd always wanted. The longing was for a girl, and a girl she received. With the return of the dark and the cold of winter, a new voice echoed inside the castle walls. At last, her life had come full circle, and no matter what was to occur, she felt whole like never before. With the child's arrival, there came a sense that all truth should be known. Of an evening, he was told everything, and at first thought it all so fanciful that he took to laughter and held the face of his beloved, wondrous storyteller. Only when she demonstrated her control of shadow and scare and brought a spider-thing temporarily out of suspension below did he believe. However, truth brought a distance between them for the very first in all their time together. She thought it would heal, but as time went by, they seemed to grow ever apart.

She'd seen this in the lives of others. Women had come to her professing of cold beds, with their love having turned the blackest burnt timber as their men stoked fires elsewhere. It was happening to her, yet all the love she needed she'd birthed, and so she deemed the loss was his. As the years went on, he'd take off on further adventures and be gone for many moons. On return, he'd keep to his own quarters, and rarely would they dine together, or anything else for that matter. She suspected another was involved, and so she turned to her old ways for answers. But there was no one else, and so what she'd known all along was the only truth of it. After their daughter's seventh birthday, she arranged for the wildfolk to take her on a journey to the shimmering lakes where they would camp and entertain her with song and wild living for a spell. At the castle, she woke her spiderfolk and gave instruction they be ready for her will to be obeyed once more. This day, she would have her talk with her one true love, and say her goodbyes forever.

She had him walk with her. Throughout the castle they swept, exchanging bitter words so in contrast to those which had filled their early life together. Not a single tear she shed. Down to the dungeon level he was taken, and when anger finally consumed him, he turned to see her standing beyond a locked iron grate. Further enraged, he demanded release and that this be the last shackle she would ever put upon him. She merely cackled at his outburst, like in the days of fell sorcery and of bargains bought and broken. When at last he calmed and talked in quiet pledge of vengeance against her, she took to sorrow for what they could have had and had never truly owned. A lever she pulled, and a grinding of stone on stone reverberated somewhere. Nothing seemed to happen, and his anger rose once more. Amid his rage and protestations, she held up a hand and would have him hear the last of it.

"Your true nature I knew when the first days of our courtship began. When you reached for me with that particular hand. Out in the wilds, given the choice, you'd always choose the lefthand path to explore. Subtle in other ways too, did your heart reveal itself to me. In talks of our future, you were distant and remote, never committing to any plan or promise. When the gift of a daughter was ours, I knew she meant lesser to you than she does to myself."

He looked everywhere but at her.

"You see, I've known all along your intentions. I confess, I used you for lust and for the attainment of a child. I learnt long ago about wolven men and vowed then they'd not wreck my heart again. I've never loved you … because I've never been fooled by your deceit."

Now he looked at her, as the truth was laid bare.

"Yes, that's right. I know who you serve and why you fell at my door in that winter storm way back when."

He'd been outwitted by the more seasoned adversary, and now the last play was to feign an empty love for her.

"My sweet, I've been lost is all. It's true, I've always wanted the road beneath my feet, but I can be home now, and we can be a family together. This I vow to you, if you'll only just unlock the door."

His eyes were pleading, and a slight smile crept onto his face. Distracted, she glanced at her surroundings, then answered him.

"Do you like this chamber? My father had it built long ago. It served its purpose well in dealing with his enemies. And, now … after a long spell of neglect, it can be counted on by his daughter too."

A second lever she pulled, and the floor on which he stood began a slow tilt. He scrambled to try and hold on to anything which would prevent a pitch into the space below; a space occupied by his killers. She'd summoned the wolves from the forest in advance, and for their queen they'd happily devour this treacherous wastrel. His plan had been to bring her pain for the crossing of the astral orphans. He was their earthly agent, tasked with giving her what her heart had desired—a child—and then taking it away in death to have her crushed for her impunity. He'd planned a poisoning, but it was all for naught, as the tearing and the rending stripped the flesh from his bones in the most harrowing end possible to his carefully crafted scheme. Love had been the thing he could not fake, like the love taking place at this moment by creatures who would not have their warden put to harm. She watched, impassive, as he came apart in the pack of her loyal subjects.

Chapter Seven

Out of dormancy, her spiderfolk removed all trace of his existence. The pale man-at-arms burnt all of his belongings on a bonfire in the grounds, and the wolves took the scraps of him back to their forest lairs. She was tired after many years of outwitting her nemeses. The grand deceivers had themselves been deceived, but it had taken a toll upon her health.

Their daughter returned shortly after to the lie that her father had gone away again, but for good this time. Only young, she knew not of the ills of their union, and knew only that she missed him so. It was a wound she'd carry into adulthood. Her mother would have no other deceit take place, and so told her all of her past and of the powers she wielded.

The terror of the spiderfolk was endured, and in time, she came to accept they would do her no harm.

For the matriarch, they'd been things of her imagination which she'd brought to life when grown, and when having the craft with which to make them. For her daughter, they were now her playthings and helped occupy her time in a place devoid of other children, and even other adults beyond the visits of the wildfolk.

The years crept by and the mother came to middle age. Her health had been a constant thorn in her side. It was the price she knew she paid for her dealings with dark forces. Now a full-grown woman, her daughter took interest in the things unearthly and would have her mother teach her so. It made good sense, for when she shook off this mortal coil there'd be a need for her successor to be able to defend these lands. These things her daughter would learn, but dark was her heart, and so dark became her art. Her path to sorcery was a necromantic branch, and it reached into those facets of nature concerned with shadow and scare. Her father's blood flowed in her veins, and the evil it carried was a strong connector with these strands to the other side.

As she advanced, her teacher grew older and one day would be gone when her time of flesh was spent. And then one day, communing with wraiths in legion with those her mother had deceived, she learnt the true fate of her father. That wound she'd carried with her was again reopened and raw, and Hell would be the price to be paid for that sorrow.

In quiet ire she seethed. It was a betrayal she could not forgive. She'd learnt not of her father's intent to murder her, the very thing her mother had protected her from. Only the knowledge of his death at her mother's hands was imparted in the hopes they'd have their final revenge in a twist of fate not even they could have foreseen. There was still much of the craft to learn if she was to best her mother. And so, cradling her fury, she swallowed that jagged pill and carried on as normal. It fuelled the thirst for knowledge, and she became more adept in weaving darkness than her mother had ever been.

Finally, the day dawned when she would confront the ailing matriarch and have her pay for her deception. By now, the spiderfolk were hers to command also, and her greater power afforded her stronger control over them. She intended not to destroy the one who'd murdered her father, choosing instead to have her become a thing of the fairy tales she'd been told so long ago. She'd have her know who she was and what she'd become, so that her suffering would be enduring to the end.

The stave was the key. Always, it was at hand with her mother. These days more so, as it offered support to the failing matriarch. Still, great care was needed as the elder, though sickly, was full of guile born of two lifetimes in this world. But there was one whom she trusted, even if it were just a little. The pale man-at-arms had been a lifelong companion, and over time, had even developed a character of his own which was endearing, if only to an ageing necromancer.

While she slept in the most empty hour of the night, under command from her daughter, he entered her chamber and took the stave. She woke that day with less defence than she was used to. In a panic, she used much of her power by loosing her will to go in search of it. That path brought her mind's eye to her smiling daughter, and revealed the evil in her heart and its ruinous intent. Broken by this revelation, it was an already defeated mother who faced down the wrath of her only child. There was no explaining which would appease her. No pleading that would turn her from her course.

The battle began in the bed chamber, but soon spilled into the rest of that fated place.

Epic it was. A contortion of powers coming together. One sought defeat, the other deflection, until love was utterly shattered and she responded in kind. Age-old wrongs infused her with the intent to fight back and overcome, but frailty and the passing of years prevented it. It came to an end in the great hall, in the seat where a coronet had been placed on her brow to symbolize her ascendancy. In the chair of knotted oak and steel, the one her father had commanded of craftsmen, she collapsed, utterly spent and at the mercy of her own flesh and blood. There was no death blow, no fatal strike to tear the life from her frame. Instead, a necromantic sleep took hold, and she slipped from a life she'd always fought to have in all fairness. The enforcer, now her daughter's, carried her limp form from the chamber, down the winding steps to the cellars, and laid her among other wares of useful nature. The victor, her grinning offspring, had followed along and now stood over what she'd make into something else.

The parts unneeded were removed and fed to the other servile creatures, save the man-at-arms. They were the offerings given in exchange for 'other pieces' which were grafted to a reimagined corporal shard. An effigy of root, twine, and dark ochre was fashioned with great care and then set to flame with the smoke blown by mouth over the motionless construct. As the hexen dolly reduced, the incantation was evoked between creeping fumes which slipped in eldritch ways into the nose and throat of it.

And so it came to pass in the grey light of early morning, that new life was born from the entrails of death, and its cries were another weeping of this dreadful place. There was a lifetime to live within this great abode, and company would be needed for that span. She would be her plaything and would do all at her behest until that time expired. Part human, part something else, she was now one of the spiderfolk from her childhood stories and made in her daughter's quest for vengeance.

The Tangled Web We Weave

In this wretched form, the former maid of the vale, crone, and matriarch was made to serve her daughter. The site became one of evil, not simply of revenge as it had been so. An awareness of who she'd been was dim, but over time, in the company of the pale man-at-arms, she gained much in the way of recollection.

The wildfolk left the region. No longer under her protection, they'd feared her successor and were right to do so. Any and all who had been loyal to her mother were branded for persecution. Ghastly things undead she sent in pursuit of the gypsies. But gifted with sixth sense, they'd foreseen disaster and returned to ancestral lands ahead of her wage upon them.

She'd raged at such an empty outcome and turned that wrath upon the denizens of the great forest. In the dry autumn, she put flame to it and scorched the earth so that those which did not perish in the fires could not return to the graveyard of nature's cradle.

The vale was now a totally lifeless shell. With the township long gone and its wild spaces nothing more than parched tracts, the hinterland was a place of foreboding and despair. To the world around it, its many stories became those to tell around campfires or as warnings to children. Behind the dense walls of the castle, the necromancer became ever more powerful and fostered a darker bond with the misfits of heaven. In such a way, she became invincible and was sought out by kings and dark lords bent on dominance and treachery. High was the price for the ration of her power they received, but in their greed they took the deal and paid later in spirit.

All the while, a certain minion that was almost forgotten crept with design in mind through the bowels of the stronghold. Long had been the fashioning of its plan, but short would be its execution.

In a time of much undertaking, the conjurer would spend long hours in her witching chamber and not see servant nor daylight for days. During one such span of time, the creature-mother made its way down to the cellars and set to work using the tool it had been given in the zeal of its creation. The want of a certain punishment had overlooked the potential that form could bring. A recalling of knowledge over the years, combined with an ability to cocoon and transform, was put to good use.

There, in the darkness and the damp, a means to change was spun and suspended from the rafters, and voice given to an incantation remembered. And then, in mandibles, a single link from old chainmail hung in the armoury was taken inside, as its element would be needed.

When done, a fat, writhing chrysalis hung suspended by morbid threads, which vibrated on the pulse of the thing inside. A translucent wall revealed a thrash of limbs within which moved through an egg-white liquid and brought the face, on occasion, to the surface. The creature was in the grip of another transformation; one of change and strange acceleration.

As day began a fall away to dusk, activity in the cocoon grew still. It no longer throbbed with hidden purpose, but merely vibrated every now and then in eerie ways. Threads as thick as stout cord kept the sack a good measure from the floor. As the last ray of light dipped below the horizon, and when darkness stole in to claim all as its own, a single fingernail pierced the cocoon wall from within, and the pus of suspension began a slow spill. The first of it was foul spatters, followed by a steady pour which dripped to the floor to form a rancid pool. The prelude to an unspeakable emergence, it was slight in comparison to that which followed. She birthed in an explosion of the rage she'd kept hidden.

Her howl swept upwards through the bones of the castle as the cocoon tore apart and delivered her unto darkness again. The necromancer, immersed in the work of shadow and scare, knew not of what transpired in the womb of her lair.

Out of sight in the gloom of the depths, her mother came upright in the mirror image of the pale man-at-arms. She was a thing of majestic revulsion. A hybridisation of woman, spider, and armour plating, she stood tall in stature, wide in brute strength, and bore a face of comely death. A vision of the supernatural, she had long, flaxen hair, and orbs with vibrant teal irises ringed by a darker hue. Her skin seemed as hoarfrost, and the facial features were the fine lines of a comely rogue. It was a design to evoke fear, and, though outlandish when in open form, looked no different from a fully armoured soldier when all legs were tucked and sited for human guise.

The chainmail ring's metal had provided the ingredient for the all-over tensile sheath, and as the conjurer surveyed her handiwork, she used water from a barrel she'd placed there earlier to wash herself clean. All that remained was to furnish herself with the stave which had been taken from her, and she'd be ready to face her human opponent.

For this, she communed with her old enforcer, and with guile he retrieved that which he'd stolen from her in service to another. Her new form was pleasing to him, and for the first time ever, his to her. In that moment, they knew there would be something between them, but for now, the problem of the new necromancer remained. It would be a battle more epic than the last, but with stave to hand, she stood a good chance of dealing death to her daughter. Through all the secret ways of the castle they kept to stealth before taking to hiding places outside the witching chamber and waiting for the hour when she would emerge. Part arachnid, it was inherent to their nature, and so the long spell of time mattered not. For a full day they lurked in the shadows, until at last the door latch broke the stillness of the corridor. Looking weary, the daughter emerged and took a slow pace along the vaulted channel. When she turned a corner, they gave creeping pursuit.

At the intersection, she had gone out of sight as if their presence had been known to her. The chance of ambush was lost, and the matriarch knew she'd now have to face her in open conflict. She told her enforcer to shadow her, and keep that distance until the key moment of combat. He nodded and looked on as she went on the hunt for her offspring. There would be a need for food and sleep, or both, and so she went off to the kitchens first. No noise could be heard from those two chambers, so stairs she took to restful quarters. Each step part of the countdown to a grim encounter, she made it only halfway up before the air charged with black lightning and arced to strike her breastplate. It danced over the rest of her as she was slammed against the outer wall and pitched forward over the open spiral to go crashing below. A ragged scar ran down the metal where the bolt had hit her protective exoskeleton, and the same had saved her from the damage of a brutal fall.

In swift response, all limbs flipped her upright, and she vanished in a burst of cawing ravens which took flight from their pursuer.

It spilt out into the courtyard as she rematerialised with her daughter mere steps behind. A volley of energy was discharged by both, which came together in a punch of power to emit a shock wave which threw both of them off their feet. The boom echoed throughout the stone structure and gave clamour to an empty hinterland. With extra dexterity, the matriarch was first to stand, and used that advantage to give voice to another offensive spell. In answer, vines split away from walls and overgrown cobbles underfoot to find their target and wrap the body at speed. But it was not quick enough, as the daughter loosed her own countermeasure before the tendrils could pin her arms and prevent the use of stave. They burnt away in rapid reduction and fell to ash as she took a moment to look her mother up and down and register the transformation. A dawning of the mistake she'd made in what she'd deemed a punishment hit home. They side-stepped in a slow circle of each other and uttered words of ruin before the onslaught of death magic to come.

"I should have just destroyed you and fed your vile carcass to the other creeping subordinates you made."

The woman-at-arms simply hissed and spat venomous spittle at her feet.

"But then again, there would have been no pleasure in it. I've enjoyed watching you bring me every kind of this and that and cower when you've displeased me. I think with what is left of you today I'll make a more simple slave, and confine your servitude to the garderobe and cesspit."

"To think that once you were my very reason to live. I know now you were a mistake and one I plan to rid from this cursed bloodline. I think you'll find me more an adversary this day than when we clashed back then."

"Then put your guard up, Mother. Destruction is coming, and I wouldn't want it to be a thing over so swift."

She brought a writhing, black fire which her mother quelled with a barbarous hoarfrost. The two produced a mist which hung a short while and then dissipated. Through it, they lanced at each other with probing strikes which tested the defences of the opposition. The mother was indeed a more dangerous adversary this time around. All manner of wraith and gaunt spectre were summoned to bring about the downfall of the other, but on they waged, cancelling each other out in the bid for supremacy. But then at last, using trickery unknown to the elder, her daughter gave conjure to a spore-rot which quickly ravaged her stave to disintegration. Without this tool of focus, she was hindered badly, and the advantage swung against her in an instant. A volley of molten bolts followed in quick succession, and, pinned down against the outer wall of the castle's defences, she was buried beneath a cascade of falling stone. Dust swirled up in the aftermath, and the victor walked through it to make good her demise.

A final build of energy was fashioned, yet before she could release it, the rubble vibrated, then flew apart as the matriarch used the brute strength of her newfound form and sent it hurtling from her as she rose in a blistering attack. Her plate had protected her, and now comely features peeled back to reveal the jaws of the true thing within which buried its fangs into the shoulder of its target. She howled through the plunging pain and was hauled high, but soaked up the damage and went to level her stave for the last unleash of annihilation. Until her wrist met with resistance, and a crushing pressure forced the conjurer's cane to fall from her hand. As it clattered on the cobblestones, she turned and looked up at the other thing which now held her and commanded the pale man-at-arms to unhand her. In response, his handsome features peeled back and he too sank his fangs into the opposite shoulder. With an arm apiece, and a firm bite to her frame, they wasted no time in delivering a killer combination.

Their muscles clenched in a split-second of preparation, and in that moment the daughter understood what was about to happen. Her scream was curtailed by a crack like breaking pottery, at which a gush of crimson welled up out of her nose and throat. As they pulled with all their might, there was a rasping tear which saw her shoulder, head, and spine go one way and the rest of the torso the other. The rending continued down until she came utterly apart. Guts and dark heart dropped from the rags of flesh and bone, and the spray washed walls and yard with her blood. Dropping her half of the remains, the matriarch whispered a fell incantation over them for a malediction which had yet to bear fruit. The grim history of this site was at an end, and in the death of her daughter, the want to be here was over. She now knew what her destiny had been all along. It was never in the world of men. Fate had ejected her from that realm, but it had taken a return to understand why that goal had been necessary. There could never have been a man or a child for her unless she made that possibility in an altogether different way.

On winter's return, they made the castle the stuff of memory and decay. The pale man-at-arms put a torch to oil throughout, and they stood in the grounds and watched it roar like a giant furnace. Hybrid spider servants had been undone with magic, and their remnants turned to ash along with those of the evil necromancer. Carrying what little they needed, the pair took a crooked lane amid falling snow and disappeared through the spindrift. A blackened, charred thing, the castle stood a broken gravestone marker to an age best forgotten, lest it evoke unwanted nightmare. It would fall into further ruin in the sorrowful rake of time—a haunted place, and ever the snare of a tormented soul forced to inhabit those blighted walls by the curse which had been laid upon her. As the world grew up around it, the vale would become a smaller, forgotten place which would slip into lore and find its way into tales of mythic proportion. Ghostly sightings at the faded stronghold would become stories spread far and wide by those who'd see her phantom on their travels through the region.

As for the pair brought together by strange fate and sorcery, they took the old fen road to the edge of what had been the great forest. There were traces here and there of nature making a reclamation of the once lush ground. Ice-bound and beneath a blanket of snow, it was hard to know how well a recovery was happening. But in these signs there was hope, and she carried it with her into the caves in which they descended. They'd been her home once before, and they would again in the building of a new life in her beloved wilds.

Her once enforcer, now lover, set about the making of a labyrinthine complex within the lungs of the mountain. Aided by strength, unending stamina, and her black magic, it was done before the last icy fingers of the season withdrew from the land. A series of woven chambers all connected by strands as thick as stout cord and interspaced too by wooden gantries filled the once aching hollowness of the depths. They could enjoy the vastness of their lair no matter what form they chose to move around within the space. With her bend of natural forces, she put energy into his handcrafted lanterns which he'd hung at interval throughout. They would ignite and extinguish upon command and could shine endlessly if left unattended. It was like a township inhabited by two ... but not for much longer. Her first batch of child-spiderlings took only months to emerge from their egg sacs. Within a year, their progeny had populated the entire cave network, and her home ... her true home, was filled with the bustle and vibrancy of life. Everything about this way of living felt right to her. The love was real, and their home was a part of nature, not removed from it like in the domain of men. As their nest grew, it evolved in design as each new wave of offspring added their own flare to the structure. Males brought additions to the build, whilst their female counterparts provided even more artistic accompaniments.

As the seasons roared by in their myriad of colours, she went from matriarch to crone again in her twilight years. Her span of ageing in this form was prolonged by the cement of sorcery and doubled what would have been her entitlement. In those latter days, she took to writing down the events of her many lives using crow feather and ink to record what had passed in handmade journals. It read like an unbelievable fairy tale, and every now and then, she'd read another chapter to a gathered multitude before bedtime. In this way, each generation learned of the folly of men and of their dark deeds, and of a way which had nothing to do with nature. Outside their cavern complex, a new cover of trees and shrubs had grown to replace the great forest. Not as dense or vast, it was, however, a burgeoning home to returning wildlife. To her kind, it was known as the mirkwood, for it shrouded their existence, and kept them safe from the outside world.

One day whilst admiring her mate, their children, and the haven they'd created, she thought it poignant how she and those around her had become the spiderfolk her mother had told her of in fairy tales. Rich in love and successors, she had finally inherited a kingdom no mere mortal could take away. The warlock who'd saved her from certain death all those decades ago had seen her future in the flight of birds and in the winding of the water. He'd offered her not prediction, but instead the means to make it so.

She came to realise it had been the greatest gift bestowed upon her, for it had made all she had now the reality it was. In her children, she saw the unfettered drive of her will and the deadly presence of her soulmate. These facets pleased her, for she knew they would be traits which would keep them all safe when the elder pair were placed at rest. Those gifted in the art she trained well, and in blade and bite her old enforcer taught them true in equal measure.

But in truth, there were no more enemies left to fight. The days of wrath and ruin were consigned to legend, and her passing would mark the culmination of an era. When first put to flight in her youth, she had been weak and bait for any who might have a want to destroy her. In the dimming years, she was more deadly an opponent than any who'd put the vale to steel in their want for power. Long she pondered these things and came to a bargain with herself. She would face the bitterness of her past and keep its lesson close, lest she grow complacent and allow wolven men the opportunity to encircle her hard-won peace and bring the death they crave. In this acknowledgement, sometimes, in the most empty hour of the night when all her kin were in slumber, she would journey back to the dead byways of the vale and take a stroll through the broken boundary walls of the crumbling stronghold. Enchanted moonlight would set down a path for her to follow in its lure to have her see the haunter of a cage of her own making.

Gossamer despair was she. Cold stone the trap in damning artifice with a spellbinding her mother had nailed into her soul. All things of shadow and scare surrounded her, but none were bound to her control. Instead, they tormented her, and would for an aeon yet to be counted. Between this world and the next, she resided in a purgatory she'd fashioned in a bid for unrelenting self-service. Her hate had festered and poured a madness into spirit which was beyond comprehension. Her mind had turned in on itself, in part to escape the ever-present dark shapes, but also from the feed of evil which was powerless to free her from her wretched confines. Such force she'd wielded, and ever was it but an inch from her grasp in the weaving of the curse that turned her seat of power into a shackle of bondage.

Beyond the veil between worlds, she'd scream at her mother and tear at her own endlessness, hoping without hope it would undo her from this bleed into nothing. Enough times her mother came to visit to make the sting deeper still in the suffering of it. On the final visit, she stood her stave against what remained of the rampart, gave whisper, and left that dread place forever.

Under sentinel stars, an ethereal hand sought to reach for it. Through force of will and fragmented memory of spellcraft, the owner of that grasping limb took hold of the key which would unlock her cage. Pulled by arcana from one realm to another, it warmed a cold palm in a dizzying moment of victory. Quickly primed and hoisted to useful position, it was promptly invaded with spore-rot which ravaged it to the point of disintegration. A totally crushing move in an unending malediction, it was her mother's way of saying one last goodbye. The scream echoed through the vale but was heard only by the one who'd evoked it. As the mother reached the tree-lined border, she cast one final look over her shoulder at the world of men and then slipped into the cover of the mirkwood. The pre-dawn walk through its eerie gloom was soothing, and she took to thoughts of human nature. Many were her ponderings, but one aspect she fully understood. Always was there a need to grasp, like that which had just taken place in the faded fort. She was guilty of it herself, but had lived long enough to learn the recklessness of it. So many lives laid low in the want for want itself. Once, long ago, her heart had been poisoned by such blind desire, and those opposing her had come to know the little of their worth in the grimdark strands of the spinneret.

In the thin, grey light of sunrise, she descended into the heart of the mountain and made a silent vow to never leave her lair, lest it be to keep the wolven men from her door.

Epilogue

There was no one left in the vale to live happily ever after, save the one who lived far from the eyes of men. And it should be known, lest any and all forget, that a woman's suffering is a visceral thing. The want for revenge is quite another. Together, they can evoke the rise of a primitive passion. But in dark craft combined, with the control of one who walks between worlds, these things can be made manifest and become a vessel of retribution to howl from the beyond.

The End

About the Author

Keith Anthony Baird is the author of *The Jesus Man: A Post-Apocalyptic Tale of Horror* (Novel), *Nexilexicon* (Novel), *And a Dark Horse Dreamt of Nightmares* (Book of Shorts), *This Will Break Every Bone In Your Heart* (Novelette) and *Snake Charmer Blues* (Short), and a psychological/horror novella titled *A Seed in a Soil of Sorrow*. His works can be found on Amazon and Audible.

He is currently querying a dystopian/cyberpunk novella titled *SIN:THETICA*.

The *Diabolica Britannica* horror anthology was his brainchild, in which you'll find his own contribution, *Walked a Pale Horse on Celtic Frost*. 2021 saw the release of the *Diabolica Americana* and *HEX-PERIMENTS* anthologies, the latter in partnership with author Ross Jeffery.

He lives in Cumbria, in the United Kingdom, on the edge of the Lake District National Park.

Twitter - https://twitter.com/kabauthor

Acknowledgements

Ann, family and friends, author pals, and everyone who makes up the horror community. Steve and Heather of Brigids Gate Press for believing in my work. Elizabeth for the fantastic art. Lastly, John Weston, my old English teacher, for seeing what others could not at the time. My heartfelt thanks to all.

CONTENT WARNINGS

Child murder
Some graphic violence
Sexual content
Rape

More From Brigids Gate Press

Visit our website at www.brigidsgatepress.com

Medusa.
Cursed by the gods.
Slain by Perseus.
A monster.

So the poets sang.

The poets got it wrong.

Daughter of Sarpedon: A Tempered Tales Collection is an anthology of short stories, poems, and drabbles, ranging from retellings to completely new stories, from ancient to modern day.

A Quaint and Curious Volume of Gothic Tales; 23 stories of madness, pain, ghosts, curses, unspoken secrets, greed, murder, and one of the creepiest collections of dolls ever. Ranging from traditional gothic themes to more modern tropes, this anthology is sure to please the reader… and send a cold shiver or two down their spine.

So, come on in; enter the parlor, find a place by the fire, and experience the beautiful, dark, and occasionally heartbreaking stories told by the authors. The editor, Alex Woodroe, has passionately and carefully curated a powerful volume of stories, written by an amazing and diverse group of contemporary women writers.

Return to the Weald, the world Stephanie Ellis introduced us to in The Five Turns of the Wheel.

Reborn is the story of Cernunnos, the Father of all, who has risen. Born of blood offerings, he travels to the Layerings—one of those places, like Umbra, which sit just beyond the human veil.

Reborn is the story of Tommy, Betty and Fiddler, the infamous troupe whose bloody rituals were halted by Megan, Tommy's Daughter. Rendered weak by Megan's refusal to allow them to hunt in the human world of the Weald, they seek their rebirth and forgiveness from the Mother and Cernunnos.

Reborn is the story of Megan, who follows Cernunnos and Hweol's sons on a pilgrimage of hope—one that would see her husband restored to her and the dark presence of Hweol removed.

Ultimately, though, Reborn is the story of Betty, the most monstrous of the three brothers. He is Nature, red in tooth and claw. He is what the Mother made him. And who are we to judge?

s delivers another powerful tale of folk horror that will captivate the reader from the first page until its final bloody climax.

Arthur, whose life was devastated by the brutal murder of his wife, must come to terms with his diagnosis of dementia. He moves into a new home at a retirement community, and shortly after, has his life turned upside down again when his wife's ghost visits him and sends him on a quest to find her killer so her spirit can move on. With his family and his doctor concerned that his dementia is advancing, will he be able to solve the murder before his independence is permanently restricted?

A Man in Winter examines the horrors of isolation, dementia, loss, and the ghosts that come back to haunt us.